A Cry in the Moon's Light

A NOVEL BY
A L A N  M c G I L L

# A Cry in the
# MOON'S LIGHT

# ONLY LOVE DEFEATS EVIL

For those who believe in true love.

For you, the reader. Thank you for your interest in this story and taking the time to come on this adventure. It is my sincerest wish that you enjoy your time in the world contained within these pages. I hope it exceeds your expectations. May you find all the horror, mystery, suspense, and love that you expect within this tale. Thank you for allowing me to entertain you for just a short while.

# Only Love Defeats Evil

The moon rises in the night sky.
Your carriage awaits.
Travel the forest if you must,
Not knowing who to trust.

Eyes flicker in the dark.
They follow your every move.
Rangers, Highwaymen, and Hessians await.
Make haste, flee, you must reach the gate.

A castle of mystery stands its ground,
But escape you must. Go, eastward bound.
Along the sea you will find
Treachery and deceit of a kind.

He saves you again,
And carries you away.
An abandoned church for you to pray.

As night follows day,
They will need to be saved.
The black wolf has killed and will kill again
Unless he gets there to save the men.

Mystery of the Wolf,
The Secret of Silver.
A witch's brew began it all.
A cry in the moon's light is their call.

# CONTENTS

# ONE

# THE LONG, COLD RIDE

The Dark Forest was a dangerous place to travel, especially at night. The full moon had been steadily rising but would not reach its peak for a few hours. Until then, scant moonlight would filter through the trees. We'd be able to see the road, but we would need the carriage lamps to help guide us.

The night air was cold and crisp. I looked up to find a clear sky filled with a million stars. My breath clouded across my vision, white in the moonlight.

The black tricorne on my head would not be enough to keep me warm. I pulled my scarf over my mouth. It would need to cover my ears, too, once we were moving.

My gaze fell to the dark stone mansion before me. Two large torches burned on either side of the door. Dozens more lit a path down the cobblestone driveway and toward the forest. The firelight illuminated flowers that surrounded the house, their reds, purples, and yellows dulled beneath a layer of frost. The ice crystals sparkled in the torchlight.

The high, iron-framed windows featured pointed edges and sharp lines. A small glow of light appeared in most of them—candles burning behind the glass.

The horses fidgeted in the cold, stamping their hooves on the cobblestones. The clatter echoed in the night.

While I waited, I inspected the team's harnesses. It was a long journey here, so last night I stopped in an open field to polish the buckles and apply a nice oil to the leather. Tonight, beneath the light of the moon and stars, it all shone.

As did the carriage. Its four lamps—one on each corner—provided the light that would guide our journey and highlighted the polished carriage. Its black finish reflected like a mirror. Glass panels gleamed in the doors and a big window to the rear. I had wanted them spotless for this trip, so I had cleaned them too.

Not many carriages had these luxuries. A carriage this expensive was meant for wealthy aristocrats who could afford it. And our company was happy to provide the service.

As I looked beyond the driveway and down the road, I spotted two blue dots glowing in the darkness. *What the hell are those?* I thought. They were a bit faint but definitely there.

Then, suddenly, they disappeared from sight. I rubbed my eyes and squinted to get a better look. But they were gone.

*I must be seeing things*, I thought. *It couldn't have been an animal. Their eyes are yellow or brown. Anything evil would surely be red, maybe black. What the hell shone blue? Road agents and highwaymen wouldn't venture so close to the house. There are much better places for an ambush along the road.*

The clanging of bolts drew my attention to the manor. Wooden doors cracked open, spilling light onto the wide stone steps. A figure stepped outside, her feminine shape all but hidden under a crimson cape lined with white fur.

A man—the husband, I assumed—stood inside the entrance. The woman kissed his cheek. The cold air carried the sound of her voice as she said goodbye. She told him not to worry. She would send word once she arrived.

She made her way down the long steps, her cape flowing behind her. The hood cast shadows across her face, masking her visage.

As she approached the carriage, I opened the door. She reached out with a white-gloved hand for me to help her get in.

"Good evening, mi Lady," I said, bowing slightly before taking her hand.

She nodded shyly and smiled. Up close, I could see how lovely she was. Auburn hair cascaded around her face under the hood. Her small features and reserved smile could melt a man's heart. But there was something else about her, an intangible quality that made it hard not to stare.

Everything was elegant: the way she dressed, the way she moved, and the way she carried herself. Even the perfume she wore allured. The sweet aroma wasn't overbearing, yet it would stay with me. If I smelled it again, I would recognize her.

"Thank you," she said, handing me her bag. She slid into the carriage.

I shut the door and latched it carefully. Once I had secured her bag on the carriage rack, I stepped up into the driver's seat. I gave a quick snap of the reins to draw the team's attention. A second snap, and we set off.

We moved slowly at first. The coach was heavier than the average carriage, so it took more effort for the horses to pull it into motion. The heft provided more stability once we got going.

Waiting outside the mansion had left the horses cold and anxious for action. But now they moved along at a nice clip. Moonlight and our carriage lamps brightened the road. We made our way down the driveway and onto the road that split the forest ahead.

I took one last look at the mansion. The glow from the windows and outside torches faded as we slipped under the tree cover.

It was certainly chilly tonight, and it got colder as we moved along. The wind froze my nose. I pulled up my scarf, covering as much of my face as I could without obstructing my vision.

My face warmed beneath the fabric. It was a welcome reprieve from the cold wind, though nothing compared with the enclosed coach. Its glass windows made for a very comfortable ride. At least, that's what I imagined—I never got to ride inside.

I hadn't even slept in it during the trip here. I'd built a fire close by and slept under the carriage so I wouldn't dirty the interior. It was lavish, lined with a lush red velour, trimmed in gold, and embellished with handles made of shiny, solid brass. The company spared no expense to make its clients feel right at home.

It was a lot more comfortable than the hard wooden bench I was sitting on. Oh, I had a driver's pad, but it was nothing compared with the extra-cushioned seats inside. *Must be nice*, I thought.

My family was poor, so this was as close as I would come to riding in one. But I wasn't complaining. If it weren't for this job, I would never get to see the country.

When I was little, I would dream about faraway places and countless adventures. My family couldn't afford to visit the backcountry or explore our lands. We didn't have a second home. Our house in the city was all we could afford. I would listen to men tell stories about their adventures and dream of having my own one day. Now, I was getting paid to travel—sort of, anyway.

I had been dispatched to take this lady to the city of Trevordeaux at the eastern border of the country. Something about a sick relative she was going to visit. It was a considerable distance from the mansion and would be a long journey.

It was urgent that she arrive as quickly as possible. My company had told me to use the quickest route. Because of this, I planned to take us straight through the middle of the Dark Forest.

There was a road to the north that went around the forest, but it added extra days to the trip. The most direct route was right through the middle. The forest road had large ruts and was not maintained. It would not be as pleasant a ride.

There were only a couple of stops this way. The first was the hidden village of Mercel, which sat a little less than halfway to our destination. I'd been told to go nonstop, but it was a long way from the mansion to

Trevordeaux and I would be running the team hard. They would need a break.

There wasn't much after Mercel either, only the small seaport town of Port Calibre. And it could be rough. So Mercel would have to do. The horses could get straw and oats. Once we left the village, I planned to ride straight to Trevordeaux.

Mercel wasn't on most maps, although people seemed to know where it was. My boss said there were a few houses, some stables, a handful of merchants, and a small inn with a pub and eatery in its basement.

The whole place sounded bare bones. None of the roads would be stoned, and I anticipated ruts full of mud and muck. The village wouldn't have any defenses either. The townsfolk wouldn't have much in the way of protection. There would be few weapons other than what the criminal element carried.

And there *would* be a criminal element. The town was in the middle of the wild country. Mercel had a reputation as a hangout for the wrong kind and a place for brave travelers to stop for food and rest.

My boss said there was virtually no type of authority. An informal town, it wasn't really recognized by anyone. It had a bunch of elders but no constable or lawman. That could be an issue. I was solely responsible for the safety of my fare.

Still, it didn't necessarily mean we'd run into trouble. Nobody in Mercel was rich, and everyone wanted the goods and services to be available, so even the criminals kept crime to a minimum inside the village. I would need to keep a watchful eye and make sure to depart at the first sign of trouble.

I hoped my passenger wouldn't mind the layover. She was in a hurry to get to Trevordeaux. She didn't seem like the snobby type, but I doubted she was used to hanging around plain townsfolk either. I was sure her nights were filled with fancy dinner parties and dances, not dinner in a dusky pub in the basement of a run-down inn.

She would be an attractive mark for any road agents or highwaymen. Her beautiful cape and expensive perfume gave her away. She may not have carried any money on this trip, but she was worth a lot.

Nobody knew we were coming. If any shady characters spotted us—or, more accurately, spotted her—we would need to leave Mercel. Especially if it looked like she had become a target.

As we continued, darkness consumed both sides of the road. Little moonlight filtered through the canopy, and soon only the carriage lamps lit the way. They lit a floor of ferns alongside the road and large trunks belonging to towering trees.

It was a peaceful ride. The air smelled of pine and oak. It was quiet aside from the occasional owl or crickets. The clickety-clack of the carriage drowned out most noise.

My mind had been wandering, which seemed to help pass the time. As I looked around, two flashes of blue in the darkness caught my eye. They looked like the same blue dots I'd noticed at the mansion. They had the same strange glow about them.

An unease crept its way into my mind. We had traveled quite a way from the mansion, yet the blue dots had stayed with us. I didn't know what they were, and that was starting to worry me.

The night seemed unending. I'd had a long ride from my company stables to my passenger's house, nearly an hour's wait before she came out. I was cold. And I hadn't eaten dinner yet, so now I was hungry. That alone made me edgy. I didn't need these blue eyes making it worse.

Water and mud splashed high in the air, cast up as the horses galloped through a puddle, and I refocused my attention. When we left the mansion, I had started them at a trot. It was a considerable distance to Mercel, and I didn't want to tire them too quickly. Plus, I wanted the ride to be comfortable. The faster they went, the more bumps we would feel along the way.

Their pace had quickened over the last couple of miles. Their nostrils flared, their massive lungs exhaling powerful breaths. It was like they sensed danger—as if they were in a hurry to get out of the forest.

I slid over to the edge of my seat, looking down into the coach. The lady sat next to the window, its curtain drawn open. Her eyes scanned the forest, landing on the full moon when it peeked through the canopy.

She appeared content, showing no signs of discomfort from our quickened pace. The carriage suspension kept her from bouncing around.

Relieved, I focused on guiding the horses around a turn. The roughness of the road started to smooth, and the tree line began to thin. Moonlight blanketed the forest, revealing open fields with tall grasses.

I was glad to make it to this part of the forest. According to the map, there weren't many open areas like this one. I imagined it would be rough terrain the rest of the way.

I had never been in this part of the country. The map I used to plot our course didn't show much. There was the expanse of trees, an odd place where Mercel was supposed to be, and a few open areas. We were looking at mostly forest until Port Calibre.

The trees parted to reveal brown grass fields on either side of the road. The moonlight fell on a scattering of small wildflowers. Without a covering of frost, the vibrant reds, purples, and yellows stood out against the dull fields. They were gemstones of color beneath a dark sky and beside a dark forest.

Ahead, a small stream meandered its way through the fields. It would be a good place to take a break; it was far enough from the edge of the forest that I would be able to see anything coming out of the woods. Knowing that nothing could sneak up on us made me more comfortable about stopping.

I pulled back on the reins to slow us down. The team came to a stop, and I locked the brake to jump down. I cracked open the door. "I need to water the horses, mademoiselle. With your permission, of course."

She didn't speak, just nodded shyly and smiled. I returned the smile and reached up to unlock the brake I had just set. I would have to roll the team forward so each horse could take a turn at the creek.

My palm landed on the warm neck of the lead horse. A born leader who enjoyed running at night, Arca was smart and liked being out front. It was why I had put him in the front left position.

He was a magnificent black stallion with a white patch above his left eye. That birthmark made him too flawed for the show ring, but that was the only flaw he had. He was muscular and strong, with powerful lungs and a gait that rivaled the best show horses. It was as if he had an endless supply of stamina because he never seemed to tire.

Killian, another black stallion, stood beside him. He shared Arca's stamina and was almost as big. But he was younger and more aggressive than Arca, with an impulsive streak. It would be a few years before he could lead. Still, Killian was full of spirit, and the two worked well together to keep everything running smoothly.

I grabbed Arca's halter and led the team to the creek. Arca quickly lapped up the fresh water. Killian waited, keeping a watchful eye on the road. Arca stayed alert as Killian drank. They often took turns watching out for the team, but something about the behavior was different tonight.

Before I could think too much about it, the coach door opened and mi Lady stepped out. She cleared the carriage as Killian finished drinking, so I pulled the team forward to let the second-row horses drink. Once they were in position, I locked the coach's brake again. I didn't want the horses to spook and run off with the carriage. The horses in the second row were young and less experienced. If they got frightened enough, the whole team might take off.

While the horses drank, I watched mi Lady stroll through the field, gently running her fingers across the grass. Her long red cape flowed behind her as she moved. Every now and then, she would bend down and smell a flower.

It was peaceful for a short while, but Arca become agitated. He stomped his hooves and bobbed his head. Killian and the other horses picked up on his restlessness, rocking back and forth. I was glad I had locked the carriage brake; it held them in place.

Intense uneasiness came over me. The hairs on the back of my neck stood on end, and goosebumps formed on my arms.

The horses' fidgeting worsened, and they let out puffs of air. Arca's wide eyes watched the forest. Killian couldn't see as clearly down the road as Arca, which made him more nervous. He also couldn't move the locked carriage. His whinny pierced the quiet.

Mi Lady turned sharply toward the forest. My gaze followed. We both saw it at the same time.

Standing in the center of the road, at the edge of the forest, was a large wolf! It didn't move, didn't make a sound. It stared as if it wanted us to see it.

Its brown fur was hard to distinguish from the dark forest at its back. But the moon lit the field enough for me to make out the strange markings on its legs and chest. They looked like ribbons or stripes weaving in and out of one another. Although the lines were jagged, they reminded me of a thatch of a roof. The moon's light seemed to make them glow an odd blue color.

None of that was quite as unsettling as its eyes. They were a bright blue—the same blue of the dots I had seen at the mansion and later on the road. When I realized this wolf had been following us, my unease turned to fear.

Fear became terror when I followed the wolf's gaze. It wasn't paying attention to me or the horses; it had fixed its eyes on mi Lady. She noticed it, too, and remained in place, perfectly still. She had walked far enough away from the coach that it might have been able to catch her before she reached safety.

The three of us stared at one another for what seemed like an eternity. The wolf remained motionless until a slight snarl took shape, revealing large, white teeth. A long tongue slipped from the side of its mouth and ran over its lips before drawing back in.

Gathering myself from this hypnotic trance, I ran to the carriage. Tucked behind my seat was my musket. Standing on the edge of the carriage, I pulled the weapon to my shoulder and cocked the hammer to line up the shot.

I closed my right eye as I focused my left down the barrel. There was nothing there! I scanned the tree line from left to right. The road was completely clear.

The wolf had vanished.

I stepped up higher onto the carriage to get a better look. From this position, I could see across the field. There was no movement. It must have run off, back into the darkness of the forest.

I wanted to get out of here before it decided to come back. I hopped down and ran into the field. "Come on, mi Lady. We need to keep moving," I said, taking her arm.

She picked up her cape, and we rushed back to the carriage. "I don't think we are in any danger," she said when she was safely inside. "I can't explain it. I just know."

I looked at her questioningly. She peered out the back window to the place where we'd seen the wolf. There was a faraway look in her eye. Softly, she said, "I don't know what it is, but there is something about that wolf."

I closed the door and made sure the latch was secure. Without any hesitation, I hustled to the driver's seat and set the musket beside me. I took one last look around as I released the brake. The wolf was nowhere in sight.

I grabbed the reins and gave a hearty snap. Without delay, Arca led the team forward. We crossed the creek with a lot of splashing. Once the heavy carriage got rolling, it moved with ease, and the horses increased the speed. They wanted out of this place, and fast.

I didn't blame them. I wasn't sure why the lady felt there wasn't any danger. When she was standing in the field, she'd looked paralyzed with fear. That'd been the animal's goal, of course. Wolves stare prey into standing in one spot. It was almost hypnotic. When the moment was right, they would strike.

That wolf had stared intently at her, as if she were dinner. When its mouth opened to show those big, white fangs, I had been sure it would make a move. Maybe it didn't think it could catch her before she made it back to the coach.

We were lucky to have gotten out of there. The sooner we got to Mercel, the better. I just hoped my boss was right and the place really existed.

I doubted the wolf would bother us in a town. Wolves generally avoid people. They like to attack when a person is isolated. Alone on a desolate road was one thing; a village full of people was something else.

The team made it through the field with ease. I let them continue their speed, making our way through the Dark Forest. I kept a watchful eye on our sides, my musket at the ready. Nothing was going to catch me flat-footed again.

# HIDDEN VILLAGE

*T*he carriage hustled down the road through the darkness, leaving the open fields. I looked back to the field one last time. As the road bent to the south, the light coming through the trees began to fade. When the field had disappeared behind the covering of trees, I saw them again.

Behind us, against the darkness, two blue eyes stood out. The wolf had disappeared when I raised my musket, and now it was back. It continued to follow.

But we were moving fast, and the horses didn't show any signs of tiring. The blue eyes fell further into the distance. Soon I could no longer see them. There was no way the wolf would catch a team led by Arca and Killian. It was unnerving that it was still with us, but that didn't matter now.

We traveled a good while before a faint light shone up ahead. This would be the hidden village of Mercel. If it weren't for the darkness, I wouldn't have noticed its slight glow. But though the moon was full, the thick tree cover blocked its light.

We rode by the light of the carriage lamps to the village's entrance. So few trees had been removed when settling the town that it was hard to see from a distance. Homes and businesses had been built among the trees. The road ran through the center of town, with branches reaching overhead. This made everything even darker.

Nobody really knew why this town was formed, my boss had said. Most believed it was because of the location. A traveler cleared a few trees half-way through the forest and made a small camp. A place to get out of the elements for the night.

I could guess how things grew from there. Once there was a cabin, another traveler thought the site should store supplies. That turned into selling supplies. Now there was a general store.

Before anyone knew it, someone else decided to construct an inn. For a small fee, weary travelers would get a warm room, fresh sheets, and a hot meal. More important, they could take a hot bath to wash off the stink.

Some folks would've come to town on foot, but most would have traveled by horse or wagon—sometimes, if they had the money, a carriage. And because of this, another somebody saw the need for a stable. After all, horses needed rest and feed.

The owners of the stable and the store needed someplace to stay. The inn was for travelers, which meant settlers had to build homes for themselves. Now there were permanent residents along with people passing through. They all needed food and a place to unwind, so naturally a pub opened.

Permanent residences, a general store, an inn with a pub, and, last but not least, a livery with a farrier. Whether there was a formal declaration or not, the stopping point had become a small town.

Mercel was never recognized by the king. There was no charter or anything like that. It was a camp that became a village. Of course, with no lawman there, it was also a haven for road agents and highwaymen. It was a well-kept secret, a place of trade and lawlessness. And the people who occupied it liked it that way.

They had an unofficial code. The criminals didn't bother the residents, and the residents tolerated a certain amount of robbery and shenanigans. Nothing was done in excess, so murderers were hunted and hanged. Nobody wanted to draw attention to Mercel. If they did, the king might step in.

We barely slowed as we entered the village along the main road. The team rolled up to the inn with dirt and dust flying into the air. Once the carriage stopped, I set the brake and hopped off.

I glanced down the road. It was still dark with no sign of the wolf. I grabbed mi Lady's bag from the rack. When I turned back to the carriage, the blue eyes shone once again. The wolf stood down the road, not advancing. *How did he catch up to us so fast?*

Arca spotted the unnatural eyes too. He stomped his hooves a few times but wasn't overly stressed. Wolves didn't like people, so it was unlikely the wolf would enter town.

I opened the carriage door so mi Lady could step out. She followed my gaze down the road but smiled, seemingly unbothered by the eyes.

Before we got to the inn's front door, she turned to me. "You see them too? The blue eyes in the darkness?" Her smile widened as she looked back at the forest. "It seems we may have an escort for our trip."

I opened the inn door for her, meeting the eerie blue gaze one more time. I couldn't understand why she wasn't afraid. When she was standing in that field among the flowers, she must have noticed the wolf's large, white teeth. They stood out in the dark. And the way its tongue had slowly licked its lips as it stared at her was kind of creepy.

But we were here now and probably safe. There might not have been any lawmen or organized government, but there were people. Some of them were bound to have weapons, maybe muskets and pistols. At the very least, they'd have axes and knives.

She entered the inn, and I followed close behind. The place was small and run down. It was probably a thriving business once, but time and neglect had taken its toll. A few crushed-velvet chairs sat in the parlor, the fabric betraying their age. The paint on the walls was faded and chipping. Water marks spotted the ceiling, suggesting a leaky roof.

I suspected this was nothing like what mi Lady was used to. Her mansion's facade had been immaculate, and I imagined the interior was no different. She would have had the best food, the best clothing, the best furniture, the best of everything. The clothes she was wearing this very night were made of the finest linens.

Though unease crossed her face, she acted as if she belonged here. She strode across the candlelit space toward a desk at the far end of the room. It held some old paper and an ink well, a feather pen with an exaggerated plume, a bell, and a sign that read *Ring for service*. Mi Lady picked up the bell and shook it.

We waited as the ring faded, but the innkeeper didn't appear. She rang the bell again, this time a little more emphatically. Still nothing happened. She tried again. The sharp ring echoed in the room and down the hall.

After the ringing subsided, we heard the muffled sound of a crowd below us. It was the noise of patrons in the basement, where the pub was located. Seemed like a bit of music too.

Mi Lady rang the bell one more time, louder. Footsteps thundered from below, nearing as someone came up the steps. The door behind the counter opened. A short man with thinning, curly red hair and a prickly beard came over. He wore a white apron and chewed annoyingly on some scrap of food.

He reached out with five chubby digits and grabbed the bell from mi Lady's hand. "Good evening, madam. We don't get many late-night visitors in these parts, I'm afraid. I presume it is your reservation that I have been holding all day and most of the night?" His voice was a thick, gruff rasp and matched his disheveled appearance. He swiveled the guest registration book toward her. "*Oui, oui*, mademoiselle. Well, of course it is. Silly question indeed. Received word of your expected arrival a few days ago. Please sign the registry, if you will."

As mi Lady signed us in, the innkeeper retrieved two skeleton keys from the wall behind him. He rounded the counter and guided us up two steps. I set her bag on the top step, thinking the innkeeper might take it for her. He eyed me up and down, then waddled past as if to suggest I was his damned bellhop.

We followed him down a long hallway. A few sconces set high on the walls gave off just enough light to see. Several doors lined each side of the hall, no doubt the guest rooms.

From the time we entered this place, mi Lady had worn a look of discomfort. It grew more intense as she followed him down the hall. But this was the only place in town, and Mercel was the only town for miles. We needed to rest before we started out again; I was too tired to travel more tonight.

The innkeeper stopped halfway down the hall and opened one of the doors. "Here ya go, mi Lady, all cozy-like. I'll be downstairs tending to the pub if you need anything. If you'll be wanting something to eat, you can get it there. It ain't much, unless you are hungry. Do join us for a drink, if you like. We have some Traveller musicians in the pub tonight, playing a bit of music to keep everyone entertained. They aren't bad, if I do say so meself. We don't get many ladies of your refined tastes in here. It would certainly brighten up the place."

The invitation was sincere, but he was also being sarcastic. He knew the kind of lady she was and that she was not accustomed to staying in a place like this. I didn't think she noticed, but I knew he was making fun of her and disrespecting her nobility.

After she entered the room, I set her bag just inside the door. I stepped back into the hall, closing her door behind me. The innkeeper looked at me again, tilted his head, and dropped the key in my open hand. A slight smirk crossed his face.

So much for him opening my door. I watched him waddle back down the hall and out of sight. The door behind the counter sounded his return the pub.

I opened my room and flopped down onto the soft bed. A fresh pitcher of water sat beside a basin on a table. I really wanted to wash up and go to sleep, but I needed to take the horses to the livery and get them settled. So I dragged myself off the bed and back down the hall.

Before I stepped out of the inn, I cautiously looked to the forest. The blue eyes were gone. I hurried to the horses, eager to get them settled. I didn't know what time it was, but knew it was late. I was hungry and tired. I needed to get something to eat and go to bed.

I settled into the driver's seat and shook the reins to get the team moving. They came to life, and we trotted off to the livery, which was near the end of town. Clouds rolled across the sky, blocking the moonlight and making it even darker.

The night air had changed since we entered the inn. It was warmer now. And it felt like it might rain, so I was lucky to get the horses inside for the night.

For the better part of an hour, I unstrapped the horses and moved each to its own stall. After that, I gave them fresh water, oats, and hay. They were all tired and hungry. Just like me.

The livery had plenty of room, so I could keep the coach inside. I felt better with it out of sight. There would be less chance of any undesirables seeing it. It was an expensive carriage. This might give the idea it was a soft target and ripe for the picking.

There wasn't anyone around this late at night. The farrier was probably in the pub by now. I would have to square up with him in the morning. Just as well, too. I wasn't in the mood to haggle about the price of grain.

I grabbed my musket from the front seat, ready to head back to the inn. As I slid the livery door shut, the howl of a wolf pierced the air. It was faint, as if from a distance, and didn't chill me like those strange blue eyes had. But it was still unnerving.

I stopped to tuck the musket under my arm and take a good look around. It was hard to see in this darkness. The trees scattered through the town created a lot of shadows.

"Kind of eerie, innit?" A voice from the dark chortled.

I damn near had a heart attack. First, a sheet of clouds turned this dark town even darker. Then the creepy howl rang out in the distance. And now someone was speaking from the shadows.

An old man emerged from the darkness. He had a long white beard and hair to match. The embers of his pipe glowed as he sucked in a big breath. When he exhaled, a billowy puff of smoke circled his hat. "Seems like the wolves have suddenly become interested in our little village, eh? Especially since you all arrived."

I didn't respond. I just shrugged my shoulders, caught my breath, and began walking quickly back to the inn. I might have been tired, but now I needed a drink. After I secured the musket in my room, I went back outside. It was still dark and hard to see, but I knew where to find the pub door. I had seen it when we rolled up to the inn. I rounded the corner of the building and slipped down an alley. A small sign hung above the stairs that led to the pub.

I made my way down the stairs, at the base of which stood a wooden door. Damn thing was heavy, and it creaked as I opened it. It slammed closed behind me. At the sound, the music stopped and everyone turned to stare.

I was too tired and hungry to care. At least I was inside now— and with lots of people around. And these were my kind of people. Ordinary. No false pretenses. No airs of importance. Just simple folk laughing and enjoying their time with a drink or two.

They quickly lost interest in me, and the music started again. Three musicians crowded in a small space toward the back of the pub. One had a violin, another a guitar. A third was using sticks to bang on the tables. A pretty, dark-haired girl clanged the small cymbals on her fingers to the same rhythm as the stick player. She wore lots of jewelry and a long red skirt.

Occasionally they walked around as they played, and the girl carried an empty mug to collect tips.

As the musicians played some mellow music in the back, a few bar wenches hustled about, bringing customers their supper and ale. The innkeeper was behind the bar, running fresh pints to the thirsty folks gathered there.

I squeezed between two strapping fellows at the bar. I eyed the innkeeper in eager anticipation. It was time for me to get one of those pints. I had to give the chubby guy credit; before I could motion him over, he appeared in front of me with a frothy pint. The large pewter mug hit the bar with a slight thud. Foam spilled over the sides and onto the bar, leaving a distinctive ring after I picked it up.

"I'll have some supper, too, if you please," I said before taking a sip. Aah, that first sip of froth from a nice cold ale. Nothing quite like it to calm the soul. The innkeeper took my coin and disappeared into the back to relay my supper order to the cook.

Finally, I was in one of my favorite type of places in the world: a dingy, old pub. The smell of ale and pipe smoke filled the air, mingling with aromas from the kitchen. It smelled good, like slabs of charred meat, potatoes, and hunks of bread. Hearty peasant food—nothing fancy. Most patrons skipped the silverware, using their fingers to shove grub in their maws. This was more like where I grew up and, unless I missed my guess, nothing like mi Lady's background.

As I sipped more ale, enjoying the music, I took in the crowd. All manner of folk had crowded into the pub, travelers and townspeople alike.

Locals were easy to spot. Their clothing had a distinct look. A comfort in their demeanor told me they weren't far from home. And I could see they'd been here many times before.

The man at the other end of the bar held the faint odor of horse— the unmistakable smell of oats, hay, and manure. His boots were dirty with dried muck from the stables. This would be the proprietor of the livery.

He kept to himself, sipping a pint from behind a full beard. The more he drank, the less careful he was about eyeing the pretty girls. As they squeezed past him, carrying pints for customers, he leaned away from the bar to look at their backsides. A few more pints, and he would most likely get some really bad ideas about his chances with them.

At a table a few feet from the bar, a middle-aged man with a slight paunch was eating his supper and enjoying a pint. He was neat and well groomed, with slicked-back hair and a small mustache. A younger man sat beside him, face practically buried in his plate. He gobbled his meal like it might be his last. His soft blond hair flopped to the side, offering a glimpse of his face. He was a little too young for any significant facial hair—or for a pint.

They both wore soft blue shirts. Their pants were black with matching shoes. I couldn't spot a speck of dirt about them. This was the owner of the general store and his clerk, no doubt. The grocers of the town. They kept to themselves, uninterested in anything other than supper after a long day.

There were other townsfolk crowded into the space, all laughing and telling stories and slapping one another on the back. Some sat at tables, eating and enjoying themselves, while a bunch of them crammed around the bar. Everyone seemed to be in a good mood and having a grand time.

But others weren't as vivacious. They were quiet and subdued, purposely keeping to themselves. Most of them appeared a little rough compared with the rest of the crowd.

A man across the pub leaned his chair back against the wall. He drew on a long pipe. His hand covered the chamber as he inhaled, and when his fingers uncurled, the embers glowed. They lit up his face for just a moment. His skin was rough and leathery. As the embers died, the shadows would hide his face again.

A woman seated at a table next to him had long brown hair that looked like it hadn't been washed in weeks. The brim of her hat hid her face. I could only make out her straight jawline and small mouth. She wasn't dainty or frilly like the beer wenches; she looked rough.

Neither the man with the pipe nor the woman in a hat spoke. They sat quietly, watching the bustle of the pub. They were rangers and drifters, by my estimation. They didn't come from any place in particular, and they weren't going anywhere special. These road agents drifted wherever opportunity led. They were out to make a quick buck—legal or illegal, it didn't matter.

Behind me and to the left of the bar, near the back, four men sat around a small table, a pot of money piled in the middle. They were playing cards. The man sitting with his back to the wall had a sour look on his face. Obviously, he didn't like his hand.

He was dressed in some type of olive-green uniform. The saber attached to his hip glinted from under the table. A pair of pistols crossed in his belt. There were two men leaning against the wall just off to his side.

Hessians. Probably fought in the American Revolution. The British had hired soldiers like them to fight the colonists. Many returned home and became mercenaries, hired guns who'd work for anyone who could pay.

None of them looked very friendly, so I decided to avoid eye contact and returned to my ale. I didn't need any trouble from them or the highwaymen—or anybody else in this place.

I raised my mug and took another cool sip. Despite the rangers, scallywags, and Hessians, this was just what I needed. The ride from the lady's house through the woods had been stressful.

I was hoping the rest of our journey would be a lot easier. Our destination was still a long way off. We would leave early tomorrow morning. If we rode hard, we could pass Port Calibre by nightfall and reach Trevordeaux sometime that night.

I wanted to limit any additional night travel. One thing was for sure: I was not coming back this way. There was a well-traveled road to the north with plenty of open countryside. After I dropped her off in Trevordeaux, I would take the north road back to my city. It was a lot longer than the path that cut through the forest, but the odds of trouble were a lot less.

I lifted the mug for another sip, gaze still scanning the room. I was shocked to find mi Lady at a table not far from the door. I had missed her when I first came in, but there she sat, alone at a table, sipping a glass of wine. She still wore her crimson cape, but the hood was down. The basement window above her cast light on her features. She was even lovelier than I'd thought.

The hints of auburn in her chestnut hair shone in the moon's light. It flowed around her thin face. Long eyelashes accented her large brown eyes, which seemed to sparkle.

Her neckline was now exposed, and I noticed a faint scar running across her shoulder and up the side of her neck. It was long but very subtle. *Was this the souvenir of a skilled surgeon, or something else?*

I felt a little unsettled. She had as much right to be here as anyone, but if anything were to happen, I didn't think I could get her out safely. Road agents and highwaymen would keep the peace—they only attacked in desolate places and rarely in town—but there were pickpockets and thieves scattered throughout the crowd.

And who knew what the Hessians were up to? They were unpredictable, and I didn't have any idea what they were doing here. It seemed odd for soldiers or mercenaries to be in this part of the wild country, especially these guys. They were generally enemies of the French.

I gulped my ale. She noticed me looking her way and nodded in acknowledgement. A little embarrassed, I looked away for a brief second, then glanced right back at her, returning the nod.

The music became livelier, and my attention shifted to the pretty musician. She was dancing around the tables, snapping her cymbals in time with the stick player's tune. Her hips gyrated, and the metal belt hanging loosely around her waist clanged in rhythm.

The crowd was getting more into it, clapping with the song. The men were all mesmerized by her movements. One guy walked up to her, ale in hand, and moved his hips with the same motion as hers. His feet danced a jig as his gaze scanned her body.

Suddenly, she stopped dancing. Her skirt twirled back in place. The band quit playing, and the crowd hushed. The man turned and found his wife, hands on her hips and foot tapping a furious beat against the ground. Her eyes were angry, and her lip curled.

He gulped hard, then lifted his mug to take a big swig of his ale. She slapped the mug from his hand. Ale splattered his shirt, and the mug clattered against the wood floor. He cowered like a dog anticipating a beating.

"Honey, I was just dancing!" he pleaded.

The crowd burst into a raucous laughter as his wife grabbed him by the ear. She dragged him across the room, slapping and punching him the whole way. Each time she swung at him, he raised his arms to block the hit. When her fist connected, he released a loud whimper.

The entire bar was in stitches, tears of amusement falling from their eyes. They clanked their mugs, and ale sloshed all over. It was a funny sight to behold.

The wife yanked open the door, then pulled her husband by the ear to lead him through it. The door slammed shut. The crowd's laughter left with them.

They'd been gone less than a minute when the pub door opened again. Everyone's eyes moved to the door, no doubt expecting the man and his wife. Probably hoping for more of their funny antics. But that is not what we saw.

Standing in the doorway was the figure of a man. Moonlight shone down the stairs, its brightness casting him into shadow. He wore a long coat and boots. His face was shaded and tipped downward, so I couldn't make out his features.

He stood there for a moment. Then he stepped into the pub, letting the door close behind him.

Everyone in the bar stared at him. I wasn't sure what to expect, but the mood lifted. The music started, the wenches delivered supper and ale, and everyone went back to having a good time.

Almost everyone. The Hessians had watched the couple and chuckled like everybody else. When the stranger appeared, their demeanor changed. They seemed very interested in him.

The mercenaries watched the stranger as he made his way to the bar. One of the men leaned in and whispered something to the leader.

The bar crowd didn't pay the newcomer any mind, and people made room for him as he went by. The crowd's reaction, or lack thereof, told me the locals were used to him here. I was certain they knew him.

The darkness and shadows of the bar hid the stranger's face but not his eyes. They were the same brilliant blue as the lights that had followed us through the forest. The same brilliant blue as the wolf's eyes!

I leaned back against the bar and pushed my hat off my forehead, not knowing what to think. I watched as he slowly made his way past the tables. When he reached the bar, the glow went away, and his eyes returned to normal.

The stranger had medium-length blond hair and a goatee shaved to a point extending to his cheeks. His appearance was neat, and his clothes were clean. He was medium built, wearing a long black overcoat that was open in the front, revealing a white shirt. Like the locals, the man wore muted clothing, but the style set him apart. The only spot of color on him came from the crimson neckpiece that accented his garb.

They might have known him, but I could tell he wasn't a local.

He removed his gloves and set them on the bar. The innkeeper leaned in, and the man ordered something, but with the noise of the crowd, I couldn't quite hear it. The innkeeper stepped back, giving an inquisitive look. He made his way to the far end of the bar, reaching the highest shelf for an old bottle. After blowing dust off the top, he pulled the cork and grabbed a small glass. He set the glass in front of the man and poured the dark liquid.

The stranger threw a gold coin on the bar as he took a sip of his drink. He turned, looking right past everyone and directly at mi Lady. His stare was precise and deliberate. He hadn't seemed to notice her, but now I was sure he knew she was there all along.

Her large brown eyes had been watching him intently since the moment he came in. When his eyes met hers, she didn't look away. After a few moments, she looked away nervously. She began to fidget.

I could see her uneasiness. She took more sips of her drink, as if she didn't know what to do next.

The stranger's gaze didn't waver. He slowly walked in her direction, taking another sip from his cup. My body became rigid, and I leaned in that direction. But he didn't walk up to her. His gaze moved away as he passed. He set the empty glass on a table next to the door. Without a word, he made his way to the door.

She never took her eyes off him. A look of confusion crossed her face, as if she was questioning whether or not she knew him.

The road agents and highwaymen also watched him. While the rest of the bar didn't seem to care beyond his initial entrance, the Hessians kept a close eye. They had taken in everything he'd done. And it looked like they picked up on the connection he made with mi Lady.

The moment the door shut behind him, she got up to leave. The Hessians noticed that too. She stood at the door, pausing for a moment to pull her hood up, then left. The heavy door swung shut behind her with a bang.

*Where the hell was she going?* There was a staircase on the opposite side of the bar that led up to the inn. The innkeeper would let her use it. She didn't have to go outside to get back to her room if she didn't want to.

I got that same feeling of dread again. She hadn't just left after him; she was following him. Now I would have to make sure she was OK.

I gulped the rest of my pint and headed for the door. As the door was shutting behind me, I saw the Hessians gathering their things, as if they intended to follow as well.

I went up the stairs to the alley. A heavy fog had rolled through town. This was strange. When I was stabling the horses, clouds had rolled in. But when the stranger came into the bar, the moon's light was bright, not a cloud in the sky. Now the clouds were back. The atmosphere was eerie and foreboding. A wolf howled in the distance, just like when I came out of the livery. It made the hair on the back of my neck stand on end.

With the clouds covering the moon's light and the thickness of the fog, it was hard to make out my surroundings. I could barely see the ground. Neither mi Lady nor the stranger were anywhere.

I had made it to the corner of the alley, just in front of the inn, when I decided to run back inside for my musket. I raced through the front door and made my way down the hall. As I did, I caught a glimpse of mi Lady's door closing. I let out a relieved breath. I must have just missed her on the street. I wasn't sure why she took the outdoor route, but she had made it back safely. Thank God.

Since she was in her room, I could go to mine. I went through my door and flopped down on the bed. This time, I was going to sleep.

The whole trip had been exhausting. First, we were followed by the blue eyes. Then we encountered a wolf with strange markings. I heard wolves howling in the distance around the town, as if they surrounded it. Next, there were rangers, highwaymen, and Hessians in the pub.

And then there was the crazy weather. One minute the sky was clear; the next minute, clouds covered the moon. And what about that thick fog that had rolled through town? It had moved between the buildings and cascaded down the alley—almost like it was a living being. Thinking, moving, hiding things.

As I lay in bed, I realized I hadn't even gotten my supper. At this point, I didn't care. I was so exhausted that I didn't even take off my shoes or clothes. I just fell asleep right where I was.

# THREE

# THE HORROR BEGINS

A loud, bloodcurdling scream rang through my room. It was the sound of a woman in excruciating pain, and it was followed by sudden silence. A man cried out in horror.

A few moments after the screams had died, people started yelling. I could hear the pub door opening and closing. Footsteps pounded against the stairs. It sounded like a crowd of people had gathered somewhere outside, and close by.

I had been sound asleep, and I wasn't sure if I was dreaming. I sat up and tried to collect my thoughts. A loud banging sounded at my door, but I was too groggy, and my body too tired and achy, to do anything about it. As my mind raced to waken, the clamor outside got louder. The banging on my door got louder too. "Who's there?" I shouted.

"Come quick, young sir," the innkeeper responded.

Still half asleep, I stumbled my way to the door. The innkeeper was visibly shaken. He was talking so fast I could barely make out what he was saying—something about an "incident" in the alley.

I went to the window, peeling back the curtain to look out. It was still dark outside, so I couldn't have been asleep long. The moon remained behind the clouds. Several townsfolk had assembled across the street. They huddled together and seemed agitated. Their torches barely provided any light in the thick fog.

I had fallen asleep with my clothes and shoes on, so I hurried past the innkeeper and out the door toward the alley. As I got closer, I could see that some of the men were armed. Only a few had guns. Others held axes, hatchets, and pitchforks—or whatever other weapons they could find.

As I pushed through the crowd, most stepped aside. I recognized some of them from the pub. Not long ago, they had been singing and having a good time. Their merriment was gone. Their faces were pale and consumed with fear.

Once I got through the crowd, I saw why. The faint glow of their torches revealed puddles of blood. More blood covered the side of the house. Beneath the blood spatter were deep gouges. It looked as if an animal had raked its claws down the wooden siding. The slashes were too high on the house to have been made by even the tallest man here. Whatever did this must have been huge.

At the end of the house, a large wooden fence stretched across the alley, closing off the alley from the woods. The slats had been shattered, as if something had burst through it. There were hairs caught in the splintered wood. If I had to guess, I'd say something had smashed its way out to escape the alley.

The crowd's quiet murmur got louder as the townspeople's anxiety grew. Their eyes were wide, and stress showed on everyone's faces. One of the men asked what had happened.

"I heard the screams of a girl," an elderly woman said. "It sounded like fighting broke out right after. Then a man screamed. I was upstairs, so I grabbed my lantern and opened the window. When I looked down, I saw a shirtless guy standing over those poor souls. There were these strange black marks all over his arms and chest."

"What else?" a man asked.

"His pants were tattered at the bottom, and he didn't have any shoes. He was covered in blood, too." She paused and covered her mouth. "He slaughtered those people."

Another man said, "I was coming out of the pub when I heard the screams. I ran down the alley and saw this large, black, dog-like creature busting through the fence. A man ran after him. They both disappeared into the woods. They're the ones who killed and butchered these people."

"Just like he said, the black dog-like thing ran off," the old woman said. "But the guy who was standing over the bodies just looked at me and glared with these glowing blue eyes. Then he jumped through the fence and disappeared into the woods."

As she spoke, my head began to spin. Her description sounded like the stranger in the pub. I began to feel faint as my thoughts ran together. Only after the woman had finished her story did I see them.

Two bodies lay just beyond the pools of blood. Their throats had been torn open. They were nothing but gaping wounds, ripped flesh, and dripping blood. The bodies were mangled, covered in bite marks and long lacerations. Something had torn open their abdomens and pulled out their entrails. Their intestines, kidneys, and livers had spilled onto the ground.

They had died violently. It was a grizzly scene of blood, gore, and carnage. Animal attacks were often gruesome and violent, but not like this.

The eyes of the male victim were wide open, his gaze empty and lifeless. A look of shock and dismay remained permanently etched across his face. The woman lying beside him was worse.

Claws had dragged down the right side of her face, tearing half her face off. The animal had ripped out her eye. It lay a few feet from her body. Claw marks continued over her left breast. It was ripped open, the jagged tears of flesh revealing pink tissue.

She was half naked, her clothes torn to shreds and scattered around the alley. There was so much blood around her, it was hard to see the color of her clothing. Her hair was also soaked in blood, but I couldn't see whether it was auburn or brown!

My stomach turned. I spun away, pushing through the crowd and back down the alley. Clasping the side of the building, I struggled to keep from passing out. I was glad I hadn't eaten any supper; it would have come up.

As I thought about this poor woman's hair, I composed myself. Instantly, I looked back at the inn. Mi Lady had gone outside just after the stranger. I gathered myself and stumbled back toward the bodies.

The Hessians pushed through, questioning everyone. The leader knelt beside the bodies and assessed the scene. He ordered one of his men to get the horses, then led his other men through the hole in the fence to pursue the beasts.

I ran back to the inn. I burst through the door, bolted down the hall, and knocked feverishly at mi Lady's door. There was no answer, no sound. I kept knocking frantically and loudly. But still she didn't answer. Where was she? Was she inside? Or was that her mangled body in the alley?

The images of the mutilated woman kept flashing in my mind. I thought I'd seen mi Lady's door close last night. But did I imagine it? Or did she leave sometime after that?

I was just about to break down the door when the innkeeper rushed to me with the key. "Hold on, hold on," he said, opening the door.

I pushed past him, but she wasn't there. Her bag was open on the dresser. I grabbed it and ran to my room, collecting my musket. I left the innkeeper behind as I rushed out the door.

The crowd was still gathered in the alley as I ran by. The doors to the livery were open. Before I could race inside, a Hessian soldier burst out on horseback with three other horses in tow. I ran inside to find mi Lady standing next to Arca. She seemed startled by the Hessian's dramatic exit and my sudden entrance. Arca's head bobbed up and down too.

"What's going on? Is everything okay?" she asked.

I was surprised to see her—and very relieved. I was glad I did not have to return to the alley. But this was no time to waste. "We should go, mi Lady. It may not be safe here."

"Why? What do you mean, it's not safe?" she asked.

I looked at her with concern. "Mi Lady, two people have been killed."

Her face turned to shock and then fear. "Where? By whom?"

"In the alley across from the inn. It was gruesome." I paused, catching my breath. "The Hessians are giving chase to . . . something. I'm not sure what did that. Looks like some kind of large animal."

My mentioning of a large animal caught her off guard. "What makes you say that?" she asked.

"They were torn apart! It might've been a wolf. I don't know, mi Lady. Whatever did that was evil," I said as I walked past her to the carriage. I threw her bag atop and set off for the stalls to harness the horses.

As I was lighting the carriage lamps after the horses were in place, the innkeeper came running in. "What are you doing?" he asked.

"We're leaving," I said.

"I don't think that's a good idea, mademoiselle," he stated, ignoring me. "It's the middle of the night, and as you can see, a thick fog has rolled in. It will be hard to navigate through the forest like that. Traveling at night in thick fog is treacherous. You'd be well advised to wait until first light. Not to mention, there are fewer undesirables out during the day. It's very dangerous at night."

I looked back at mi Lady. "It doesn't seem all that safe around here. I think we need to get as far away from this place as possible. The horses are rested. We can make it out of the forest before something else happens."

She stopped for a moment to look at the innkeeper, then back at me. She nodded her approval to me, so I motioned for the innkeeper to open the other stable door. As he slid the door open, she got in the carriage. I secured the latch, then hopped up to my seat. Grabbing the reins, I called out for Arca and Killian to depart.

The innkeeper stood by the open door as we trotted out. I threw him the two room keys and a small pouch with some coins. He opened the bag and looked inside, pleased enough. "Castle Parlimae is about ten miles to the northeast. Take the side road that banks north. Most people there don't like visitors in the middle of the night, but if they take you in, you'll be safe!"

I gave a quick wave to him as I steered the team through the town, heading west. When we cleared the last building, I looked behind me. The fog was thick, and it didn't take long for the faint glow of the village to disappear.

The clouds still covered the moon, making the forest much darker than when we came into Mercel. The carriage's lanterns didn't do enough to let us move quickly through the darkness and fog. I was anxious to get out of town, but I pulled the reins and applied the brake to slow us down.

I might have been wrong for leaving. The town was alert, and the Hessians were giving chase to the creatures. Some of the men had guns too. Maybe it would have been better to stay.

A thundering boom halted my second-guessing. A large tree was falling! The night rang with the sound of splintering wood, branches breaking, and leaves shaking as it crashed to the ground. The force of the impact rumbled the area.

I pulled hard on the brake and pulled the reins with all my strength. Arca and Killian whinnied and reared up. The team came to a grinding halt just before the fallen tree.

I set the brake and jumped down. The horses were startled and scared, but they weren't hurt. The harnesses were intact, and there didn't appear to be any damage to the carriage.

My attention turned to the fallen tree. It was enormous, its large trunk uprooted from the ground. The top of the tree had landed across the road. It completely blocked our path. There was no way to move it and no way around. I might be able to use the horses to pull it to one side. Otherwise, I would have to turn the carriage around and return to Mercel. Both options required unbuckling the horses, which I did not want to do.

I looked down the road behind the carriage. The fog was starting to lift, but the night was still pitch black. There was something strange in the air. A feeling of dread washed over me.

My hair stood with static electricity. Goose bumps formed on my arms. The wind picked up, carrying an eerie howl on its back. This was much closer than the howls I had heard in Mercel.

The sound filled the night air. Another cry came from the darkness—then another and another.

The team stood perfectly still, frozen in fear and flashing the whites of their eyes. They faced the fallen tree, so they couldn't move forward. And the brake prevented the wheels from turning, which meant they couldn't move backward.

I quickly retrieved my musket from behind the driver's seat. Pressing it to my shoulder, I stood at the ready next to the carriage door. Mi Lady waited in the carriage with a look of fear on her face. My heart pounded.

Then I saw them. One set of yellow eyes came into view on the darkened road behind the carriage. Another appeared next to the first. I spotted another pair of the amber eyes in the forest and a fourth pair across the road in the dark. The deep yellow eyes seemed to get larger and larger as the animals moved closer. Finally, their forms began to take shape in the shadows. We were surrounded by wolves.

They regarded us with unwavering gazes as they approached. They moved slowly, taking deliberate steps in our direction. Stalking their prey. Paralyzing us with fear so they could find the right moment to strike.

The wolves crept close enough for me to see their white teeth when they snarled. Drool dripped from the side of their mouths. Their hackles were raised, and their ears stuck straight up. They were all moving together, as if organized by some telekinetic power. They moved as if by one mind, with one goal: kill us.

One wolf stood out among the pack. I spotted the black male wolf as he emerged from the darkness. He was much taller and bigger than the others. Like the other wolves, he moved slowly and deliberately, but it was clear he was directing them. This was the leader.

Looking at him, I felt the presence of evil. And nausea at the pit of my stomach. I had never been a religious person. I wore a cross around my neck, but that was out of habit or superstition. My mother had given it to me a long time ago, and I always thought of it as a lucky charm. But I didn't feel so lucky right now.

My musket might get one of them. The others would be upon me the moment I fired. The only question now was which one of them was going to take the bullet.

I would not survive their attack. Mi Lady would live only slightly longer than I. It wouldn't take long for them to break into the carriage and tear her to pieces. Our deaths would be gruesome, just like those poor souls in the alley. I trembled at the thought of being torn limb from limb. Tears flowed from my eyes as fear took over my emotions. For the first time in a long time, I began to pray.

Fear gave way to sorrow. Mi Lady would have to watch, helpless as they tore me apart. She would hear my screams, all the while knowing she was next.

At the very moment when it seemed all hope was lost, a creature of incredible size and power leapt from the shadows! Its feet hit the ground with a thunderous thud. The beast stood next to the carriage, blocking me from two of the advancing wolves. I was so startled that I stumbled backward and fell to the ground. Wide eyed and scared to death, I got up and scampered onto the carriage roof.

From here, I could see the creature's massive size. It was half man, half wolf. He had large, round shoulders that supported huge, muscular arms. At the ends of those giant arms were large hands with long claws. His enormous chest expanded with deep breaths as he prepared for battle. The beast looked invincible, and I was more afraid of him than the wolf pack.

He turned slightly, and I gazed at his profile. The wolf-like face had a long muzzle and pointed ears that stood high in the air.

A snarl escaped his mouth, and I spotted large, white teeth. His fangs were so large they may as well have been spears. His front teeth were long and pointed—and looked sharp as razors. And his jaw seemed capable of snapping a bone in two.

The beast was covered in dark fur and black markings that ran over his arms, shoulders, and chest. They looked like jagged ribbons woven in a thatch pattern. And the markings seemed to glow with a dark blue tint.

When the beast turned his head, I saw his eyes: the same bright blue as the wolf we had encountered beside the open field. Was this creature the same wolf? That wolf had the same blue-black markings. It didn't make sense. This creature was part man, and the other was all wolf.

The beast leaned aggressively toward the closest wolf and let out a large growl. He moved his head from side to side, tracking the wolves as they neared. He looked big and fearsome with his chest puffed out and the long hackles on his neck standing on end.

One of the wolves moved in even closer. The beast grabbed the wolf by the throat with one hand. He lifted the animal high in the air and then slammed it to the ground. The beast's claw squeezed the wolf's throat as it hit the earth.

Another wolf leapt in! The creature let go of the first wolf and seized the second in midair. Using the momentum, he hurled the wolf backward, smashing it into the side of the carriage.

The first wolf scrambled to its feet and clamped its jaws around the creature's thigh. The beast threw his head back and let out a cry of pain. Then he grabbed the wolf and yanked it off his leg. Flesh and blood went flying.

A look of rage swept over the beast's face. He pulled the wolf close to his face and gave a menacing snarl. The wolf's eyes widened as it came face-to-face with the monster. Saliva poured from the creature's mouth as he squeezed the wolf's throat with his claws. The neck bones snapped under the force of the beast's grip. The wolf's head went limp, and its tongue flopped out of its mouth. The creature tossed the dead animal to the side and watched the carcass skid to a stop.

Startled at the death of one of their own, the other wolves stopped their attack. They looked at each other with confusion. Then they became enraged at the loss of their kin.

It seemed they might attack again, and I was helpless atop the carriage. I caught a glimpse of my musket lying on the ground just behind the beast. I had dropped it when I scrambled up here, but if I could get it, I could take out a few of the wolves.

I started to climb down, hoping to snag it quickly and return. The beast turned around and met my eyes. He let out a menacing growl, as if to say, "Get back up there." I immediately abandoned the idea and scrambled back up to where I had been!

The wolves closed in on him, careful to stay just out of his reach so they didn't meet the same fate as their friend. They darted in and out, tempting him to make a move. Enticing him into making a mistake. It looked like they were trying to lure him away from the carriage.

They couldn't completely surround him because the coach was at his back. Arca, Killian, and the rest of the horses stamped their hooves and reared into the air. Any wolves that came too close got a horseshoe to the head.

The wolf pack's patience ran out. One wolf lunged from the side, trying to catch the beast off guard. But the creature was ready and punched the wolf squarely in the side. I could hear its ribs break. The force of the strike sent the wolf flying through the air. It crashed to the forest floor and rolled end over end. The wolf released a loud whimper.

Another wolf came at the beast from the opposite side. It barely avoided Arca's hoof as its razor-sharp teeth latched onto the back side of the beast's arm. Yet another wolf raced in, slamming into the beast's side and tearing into bone and flesh. A third wolf sank its sharp fangs into the muscle of the beast's chest.

Three wolves hung off the monster's body. Their bites were deep, shredding his flesh. Blood spurted into the air. With each bite, the beast gasped and cried out in pain. Those cries echoed through the forest.

He grabbed the wolf at his side and flung the animal deep into the darkness. With a long-clawed hand, the beast grabbed the muzzle of the wolf hanging from his chest. He pulled the wolf's mouth apart until the jaw split and the head tore in two. He flung the dead animal over the fallen tree. The body of the wolf that clenched the beast's arm swung with the motion. It was determined to hang on.

With his other hand, the beast caught the wolf by the top of the head and squeezed. The pressure and pain caused the wolf to release its bite. Once it was free, the beast slammed it to the ground and drove his fist through the body. The impact killed the wolf instantly.

The beast stooped down, leaned forward, raised his head, and let out a roar of triumph. The sound carried through the forest like a hurricane. His long teeth glowed in the dark. Blood and drool gushed from his mouth. The fight was over.

My gaze fell on the black wolf standing at the edge of the shadows. He and a couple others had never joined the fight. They had watched the entire battle, more interested in assessing the beast's weaknesses and learning from the fight.

The wolves that had survived the conflict slinked into the shadows, hurt and exhausted. Just before they disappeared between the trees, they each turned and snarled defiantly.

Still standing over the carcass of the last wolf he killed, the beast caught the gaze of the black wolf. He stepped forward, but the black wolf backed away. The beast watched as the black wolf disappeared, his coal-black fur fading as if he was never there.

Several minutes passed before the beast turned his gaze from the forest, satisfied the black wolf and his pack were gone. The air calmed, and the clouds moved away. The moon's light returned, and the forest brightened. It was as if the beast had somehow cleared the sky when he defeated the pack.

He looked up at me with those glowing blue eyes. Large teeth still gleamed from behind a slight snarl. Saliva continued to drip from the edges of his mouth.

It was hard to catch my breath. The beast could easily reach up and yank me off the roof of this carriage. My musket still lay on the ground at his feet.

But just as the sky had changed, so did the beast. His snarl faded and his eyes softened. The look of rage left his face. After a few moments, he looked almost peaceful.

His gaze dropped from me to the carriage, where he no doubt found mi Lady. He didn't approach her, though. Instead, the beast walked past the horses to the fallen tree. Each step shook under his weight and power. Not one of the horses moved. They still had whale eye, the whites visible beyond the black. But they had settled and started to calm. It was as if they understood him. Somehow, they sensed the danger had passed.

He walked to the giant tree that blocked the road, looked back at me, then pressed his shoulder against it. Battered and bloody, he pushed the massive tree aside. It took a few attempts, but he finally shoved the tree far enough out of the way that the carriage could pass. Then he stood up and looked back at the carriage.

I came down from the roof and picked up my musket. I pulled it to my shoulder, slowly taking aim at him. I was going to kill this thing before he decided to attack us.

Before I could pull the trigger, I heard the carriage door open and mi Lady step out. Soft footsteps slowly approached. As she passed me, she placed a hand over the barrel of my musket, lowering it to the ground. The whole time, she kept her eyes on the beast. He didn't take his eyes off her either.

She let go of the musket once it was pointing down and started walking toward him. I whispered, "Mademoiselle, no!"

She slowly raised her hand and motioned that it was OK. In an expression of disbelief, I heard her whisper softly to herself, "It cannot be."

She moved alongside the horses as he took a couple of steps back. She placed a calm hand over Arca's mane then turned to face the beast as she removed her hood. I watched as they stood there facing each other. Her eyes moving slowly over his battered and bloody body, examining every wound. She winced at some of the tears in his flesh.

She reached out, with slight hesitation, to touch his face. A clawed hand met hers. Tears began to well up in her eyes.

He stepped back, pausing before taking off into the woods. She watched as he faded from sight. A teardrop fell from her eye. It slowly rolled across her cheek, finding its way to the ground. I could see it falling as if in slow motion. It landed in a puddle at her feet with a small splash.

The moment the tear hit the ground, a deep howl sounded in the distance. It was a cry of sorrow. A look of pain crossed her face, as if she felt the anguish in that sound.

The mood was somber. An immense sadness hung in the air. Everything was quiet. The forest was still.

She turned, slowly walking back to the carriage. "We need to go."

Without another word, she stepped inside, shut the door, and disappeared into the shadows.

# FOUR

# CASTLE PARLIMAE

As I climbed back into the driver's seat, I wasn't sure how to feel. There were two mutilated bodies in Mercel. We'd left in a hurry to escape danger only to have our path blocked by a fallen tree.

Then a pack of wolves tried to kill us. We were saved by some beast, a creature from bedtime stories told to scare children. The half-man, half-wolf was as scary as he was heroic. He was something I never believed could exist.

And he had the same markings as the wolf we encountered beside the field. I tried to make sense of the connections: The wolf's markings and glowing blue eyes. The stranger in the pub with the same eyes. And the tale of a man with markings and blue eyes who'd been standing over the mutilated bodies in the alley.

This creature had defeated an entire wolf pack with ease. He could have killed us too. Instead, he used his power and strength to do something I didn't think was possible without horses. He pushed aside the giant tree so we could keep going.

I felt lucky to be alive. *But should I be afraid?* Everything told me this creature had been following us from mi Lady's home.

And she was hiding something. She knew this creature. Her sorrow filled the night air, heavy like the fog that blanketed the town.

I pulled on the reins gently to tell Arca and Killian to get going. I gaped at the tree as we passed—it was enormous. It amazed me to think of how strong that beast was.

The corpse of the dead wolf he'd killed lay crumpled not far from the tree. Its mouth hung open and its tongue lolled. I shook my head in disbelief. The fight had been like nothing I had ever witnessed. And yet . . . My gaze returned to the tree. Moving this giant obstruction really showed immense power. It also showed he wasn't some mindless monster. He deliberately moved the tree so we could escape.

Our pace quickened once again. The rhythm of the trotting horses and clicking carriage wheels was hypnotic. My mind filled with all kinds of thoughts. Could the stranger at the tavern be both the wolf-man and the wolf? They all had the same blue eyes. The witness in the alley described him with the same strange marks. And although the stranger never spoke to mi Lady at the pub, I was convinced they knew each other from the way he looked at her and she at him. When he left, she followed him out.

But those thoughts would have to wait. We were making good time, but I pushed the team a little harder. There didn't seem to be any danger, but the black wolf was still out there. As was the beast. I didn't know if he was friend or foe, but I wasn't taking any chances. Besides, we needed a restful sleep without any stress.

The canopy thinned, and moonlight scattered along the road. It lit the forest in a peaceful and beautiful way. I gazed into the distance, tracking curtains of light across the forest floor. Every now and then, I caught a glimpse of a few deer running at our side or grazing under the light. Other, smaller animals attempted to hide as we passed.

Beneath the squeaking of the carriage, the night came alive. An owl hooted to warn everyone we were coming. Crickets chirped their song in a steady cadence.

Before long, we approached a fork in the road. The innkeeper had told me the left branch led north to Castle Parlimae. The right continued through the deepest part of the forest, and there were no stops until you were out. I pulled slightly on the left rein to move Arca's head in that direction. He took the cue and guided the team down that path. The horses moved as one unit at a comfortable stride.

The wheels of the carriage continued their rhythmic cycle. We rolled along for several miles, taking in all the bumps and bruises the road had to offer. After a short while, the road smoothed, a sure sign we were nearing civilization. The lord of the castle would pay to care for the roads leading into the village. Supply routes needed constant upkeep to make it easier to move goods and people.

I was proven right when we emerged from the forest, getting an unobstructed view of the majestic Castle Parlimae. It rested on the side of a mountain, sitting at the top of some short foothills.

This road would take us right into the castle. The road looked as if it continued past the castle to some canyons to the west. It probably connected with the great northern road that skirted the forest.

A road directly ahead of us seemed to head east and then loop back into the forest. That would return us to our original route and lead directly to Port Calibre before the final leg to Trevordeaux.

We rode past long fields that extended from the forest to the castle—peasants' pastures. They likely grew the crops that fed everyone. A waterfall coming off the mountain to the west dumped into a fast-running creek, which emptied into the fields and irrigated the crops. By my estimate, the peasants could provide enough food to last for months.

As we got closer, a small village came into view. We passed by peasants' homes. They squatted in the shadow of the imposing castle. With the mountain at its back and a deep ravine in front, it was a nearly impenetrable fortress. The entire village could hide in there safely for long periods of time.

I craned my neck to take it all in. The moonlight illuminated its high cathedral spires. Although most of the windows shone with lamplight, the castle looked quiet. Torches lined the outside wall and lit the road to the front gate.

We'd need to cross the ravine that separated the castle wall from the road. The peasants used a drawbridge, and luckily, it was still down.

It clanged as we crossed. The noise of our wheels on the wood echoed in the gorge below.

A man was leaving the castle in a wooden cart pulled by a mule. He gave us a pretty good look as we clanked across the bridge. They must not have seen too many visitors this time of night.

When we entered the courtyard, two unfriendly guards immediately stopped us. Before I had a chance to set the brake, they started grilling me with questions. Who we were? Where were we going? Did anyone know us? Why had we come here so late at night?

I tried to explain everything, but it was hard to talk as they peppered me with questions. The guards weren't impressed with anything I had to say. It wasn't until I mentioned where I had picked up mi Lady that one of them stopped talking.

I continued to explain how we had come from mi Lady's mansion in the west and were on our way to visit her sick relative. The guard who had stopped talking ran into the castle. I was about to go into the events in Mercel when the castle door creaked opened. A man emerged with the guard in tow. He paused, trying to see who was in the coach.

Mi Lady opened the carriage door and stepped out. He immediately smiled, making his way to greet her. This was the lord of the castle. I didn't know who he was, probably some kind of baron or viscount.

As they went up the front steps together, the guard who'd come out with the lord approached me. Without any further questions, the guards ushered me to the castle stables. Clearly, the lord and mi Lady knew each other.

Funny, when the innkeeper told us to go to Castle Parlimae, she hadn't said a word. And she never indicated she knew this place was along the way. Or that we would be welcomed.

While I didn't like all the secrets, I was glad the horses could get rest. Maybe I could get some sleep this time. Most important, I wouldn't have to travel anymore tonight.

I went into the stable as the guards instructed. Once they were unbuckled, I placed each horse in its own stall. I decided to leave my musket behind the seat. We were safe here, so I wouldn't need it.

When the horses were settled, one of the guards escorted me back to the castle. Servants greeted me in the foyer and ushered me away while mi Lady spoke to the lord of the castle in an adjacent room. They led me to one of the long towers, up several flights of stairs, and into a room that looked out over the valley.

Though the servants had provided me with fresh linens for the bed and water to clean myself, I was too exhausted to fuss with either. It was so late now, and I had no idea how close it was to dawn. I just wanted to close my eyes and get some sleep without worrying about being eaten by some mythical creature.

The morning light coming through the window was warm and comforting. It awoke me rather early. I'd expected to sleep later given the kind of night we just had.

The birds were singing, and a cool breeze filled the room. A rooster crow announced the new day. I got up and went to the pitcher that the servants had left last night. The water felt good on my face and arms. It was refreshing to wipe off the grime and feel clean again.

I gazed out the window. This was one of the higher towers in the castle, giving me a good view of the valley below. The forest didn't look nearly as intimidating in the daylight. It stretched for miles in either direction. The road that led us out of the forest was easy to spot. It rode beside a long field and through the cluster of houses at the foot of this castle.

Farmers from the village were tending the fields. Horse-driven plows were making short work of rich, dark soil for next year. Other fields held crews of people picking vegetables and loading them into wagons. Other villagers bundled hay into stacks. This was all preparation for the harvest.

My gaze fell to the foot of the castle. Just beyond the ravine, a handful of farmers' wives were at home hanging rugs on a line. They swatted the rugs with rakes, sending clouds of dust into the air. Other women carried water they had collected in rain barrels on the sides of their homes.

Children hurried about, feeding farm animals. Some chickens, geese, pigs, and cows meandered about, while others had been contained in small pens. The bigger flocks of sheep and herds of cows grazed in nearby fields.

The scent of fresh baked goods wafted on the morning breeze, and I breathed deeply. When I looked closer, I spotted pies cooling on windowsills and morning breads sitting on counters.

The sounds of bustling community far below were faint, almost hushed. The village was seemingly at peace with the world, existing in perfect harmony and oblivious to the horrors we experienced last night.

Four riders on horseback suddenly emerged from the forest. They weren't riding in a panic, but the horses were moving at a fast pace. The men wore drab green garments, and when they got closer, I saw a sword hanging at the hip of the lead rider. It was the Hessians. I remembered the leader's saber from the card game at the tavern last night.

Their horses were carrying them swiftly through the fields. The brisk pace and their demeanor suggested they were on a mission. It wouldn't take long for them to cross the village and arrive at the castle.

After I finished washing, I got dressed and went to look for mi Lady. I started by knocking on the door across the hall from mine. There was no answer, so I opened it enough to poke my head into the room. Mi Lady sat in front of a mirror, brushing her hair with a faraway look in her eyes. I cleared my throat, and her gaze met mine in the mirror. She smiled, motioning me to come in.

I closed the door behind me and walked over to her. "Mi Lady, I just saw a group of men on horseback riding hard to the castle. It looked like the Hessians from last night—the ones from the tavern."

The smile disappeared from her face. She stood, turned her back to me, and said, "Please tie me."

I tied the corset tightly, completing her dress. I was about to repeat the news of the Hessians when someone knocked at the door. She looked at me with slight surprise, then went to answer the door. A maiden curtsied and said, "Lord Parlimae would like you to join him for breakfast. In the main dining hall, mademoiselle."

Mi Lady smiled kindly. "Thank you. Give us a moment, please."

As the maid left the room, I asked. "Mi Lady, what about the Hessians?"

She walked over to the desk and gathered up a few things she had placed there. She thought for a moment. Walking back to the door, she said, "Let's wait and see what happens at breakfast."

The servant led us down the long hall to the winding staircase. Tapestries and paintings adorned the tower hall. There were more decorations in the tower staircase.

We reached the bottom, emerging into the large foyer. We crossed it to get to the main dining hall. This room was bigger than most of the peasant homes in the valley outside. As with the rest of the halls, it had an assortment of paintings, tapestries, and other adornments.

There was a magnificent eighteen-chair table in the center of the room. Four silver candelabras, evenly spaced across the length, shone brightly in the morning sun.

I tipped my head to take in the mural on the ceiling: A naked woman lay under a tree in a meadow. She lay on a picnic cloth, feasting on a platter of fruit. Four fat little cherubs flew about, playing different instruments above her. Seemed a bit much, if you asked me.

The walls of the dining hall were equally overdone. They showcased numerous animal heads mounted on giant plaques, each with an engraved nameplate at its base. There was a boar with large tusks, a buffalo with thick horns, plenty of horned deer, and some elk, along with numerous birds.

Behind the lord's chair, high on the wall, was the head of a large, black wolf. It was very similar to the black wolf that attacked us last night. But this wolf seemed bigger and had silver fur around its mouth, so it was clearly older when it was killed.

Sitting at the head of the table was the lord of the castle, the same man who had greeted mi Lady last night and escorted her inside. He was a robust man with graying brown hair and a short beard. As the lord of these lands, he was well dressed, even for breakfast. He wore a formal dining coat with a green ascot.

When he saw us, he smiled and rose to greet us. His hand extended toward a chair, inviting us to join him at the table. Seated to his left were two other gentlemen, one of whom looked like his son. They did not appear as friendly or as inviting as our host. Neither of them stood or said anything.

Once we were seated, a servant entered with a silver coffee urn. Three others followed, carrying trays of fruits, dried meats, and breads. They placed the trays on the table in front of us and set out plates and dinnerware. The last servant poured coffee for everyone, then they all departed.

Lord Parlimae said, "I trust you and your servant slept well. Did you have any troubles along your journey?"

Mi Lady was about to answer when the castle doors flew open, the bang echoing in the foyer. All heads turned to see what was going on. A servant escorted two of the Hessians into the dining hall.

"May I present Colonel Voelker, my lord," the servant announced. He bowed and then returned to the foyer.

Lord Parlimae rose in greeting, as did the two men seated next to him. We followed their lead and stood as well. Colonel Voelker and his companion made their way down the long table. Voelker looked at us inquisitively. He recognized us, but the look on his face suggested he did not immediately remember us from Mercel.

As if shrugging off his curiosity, he turned to Lord Parlimae. "My lord, my companions and I have been tracking some wolves through the night. They attacked some villagers in Mercel. The trail led us through the forest and went cold not far from here. Did you experience anything unusual last night?"

Lord Parlimae extended his hand, inviting Colonel Voelker to sit. We all took our seats as well. The lord gave us a fleeting glance before refocusing on the colonel. He shook his head. "I'm afraid not, Colonel. Everything has been very quiet in this valley for quite some time. Wolves normally avoid people. We don't see many of them in the valley. Are the villagers all right?"

"No, my lord. They are most definitely not all right. A man and woman were gutted in the street. Their flesh had been chewed and partially eaten." He paused briefly. "You'll forgive me for saying so before your meal."

Most of what the colonel said was true, except the victims hadn't been partially eaten. I was about to speak up, but mi Lady silenced me by placing a firm hand on my knee under the table.

Colonel Voelker studied mi Lady. "Have we met, fräulein? You look very familiar."

"I don't believe we have, colonel. Perhaps we ran into each other in Mercel last night." She took a moment, then continued. "We stopped there briefly on our way through the Dark Forest."

Voelker's reaction changed. His question was to gauge our reaction. He must have deliberately used the term *fräulein* too. It was used for single women and was often disrespectful in nature. *Frau* would have been more respectful of a married woman like mi Lady. But he wanted to see what we would do or, more specifically, what she would do.

When mi Lady spoke again, her voice was crisp. "I will forgive your tone, Colonel, as we have not formally been introduced. My husband is Francois-Henri d'Harcourt, the fifth Duke of Harcourt and the governor of Normandy."

Lord Parlimae gave her a wry smile. It amused him that she wasn't letting Voelker intimidate her. "Did you witness any of this, my dear? The villagers being killed?"

She looked at Lord Parlimae. "I'm afraid not, my lord. Our journey was rather uneventful. The activities Colonel Voelker has described must have happened after we left."

Voelker regarded her skeptically. He was not impressed with the way she corrected him. "Very fortunate for you. Tell me, what is the nature of your business that you would travel into a darkened forest so late at night, Frau Harcourt?" he asked.

Lord Parlimae spoke up immediately. "You, sir, are coming dangerously close to another insult. As you have now been told, you are in the presence of the Duchess of Harcourt and should be mindful of your tongue."

I held my tongue, too, finally understanding her reluctance to share the events of last night. She was the Duchess of Harcourt and married to the governor of Normandy. The country was already teetering on the brink of a revolution. She didn't want any unnecessary attention or scandals.

*A duchess* . . . From the moment I picked her up, I knew she was a lady of refined tastes, but I'd had no idea the importance of her position. She was worth a lot of money. Her husband had land and title.

The mansion where we began was on the western edge of the Dark Forest. It was far from the lands of Normandy. Maybe it was the governor's second home, or maybe some other wealthy aristocrat owned it. Clearly the guards at Castle Parlimae had recognized the location as important.

The governor wouldn't travel without an armed escort. That would be as large as a small army and unable to move quickly. Getting to Trevordeaux in a hurry would have been nearly impossible.

It made sense that she had wanted to leave during the night. Her itinerary was a secret. I had designed the journey, and my boss had ordered me to keep it to myself for the security of the client. He never told me her name or title to further protect the mission.

She cast a shy look at Lord Parlimae. "It's okay, my lord. I can answer the colonel," she said, turning to Voelker. "My grandmother is very ill. I am on my way to be with her in Trevordeaux. The news of her sudden illness was a surprise. That is why we had gotten a late start and were driving straight through. I have known Lord Parlimae since I was a small child. We decided to make our way to the castle, as it is on the way to Trevordeaux."

Mi Lady wiped her mouth with a napkin and stood up. "Which I'm afraid means we must leave promptly, my lord. I thank you for your gracious hospitality." She smiled at Voelker. "It was a pleasure to meet you, Colonel. I wish you good luck with your hunting."

Voelker shot to his feet. "I'm afraid that will not be possible, Duchess. Nobody is to leave these lands until we have captured and killed the beast."

"Now, listen here," Lord Parlimae said as he stood, "I am the lord of this castle, and you will—"

"This is an order of the king. We have been commissioned to kill the beast. All subjects of the crown are to obey our directives until our mission is complete. This includes lords and governors." Voelker nodded to mi Lady and said, "And duchesses."

He pulled a parchment from his coat pocket and handed it to Lord Parlimae. Its wax seal held the king's signet. Lord Parlimae broke the seal and unrolled the document. When he was finished reading it, he handed the parchment to the man seated to his left, who I'd assumed was his son. After he'd read it, he passed it to the gentleman seated next to him.

"Very well, Colonel. But you would do well to remember I am still the lord of this castle. You will show me the respect of my position, or I shall discuss the matter with the king personally," Lord Parlimae barked.

Voelker bowed his head slightly. "Of course. I only wish to complete my mission and keep everyone safe. Now, if I may, my men and I need some rest so we may continue our hunt tonight. We shall help ourselves to some grain for our horses and quarter in your barracks."

Voelker's companion stood and followed the colonel out of the dining hall and through the front doors of the castle. When the doors closed, Lord Parlimae sat back down. He waited until mi Lady sat, then said, "I am sorry, my dear. I know you are anxious to be by your grandmother's side. But your safety must take priority right now. It appears you will have to stay at least one more night. I hope last night was acceptable."

A look of worry pinched her face, but she quickly composed herself. She bowed slightly to Lord Parlimae. "I thank you for your allowing us to stay on such short notice, my lord. We slept well. The castle is as warm as I remembered."

I waited for her to address the matter of the wolf. Lord Parlimae, his son, and the other gentleman clearly hoped for the full story; they were hanging on her every word. "I am sorry to hear of the villagers that the colonel talked about. I'm afraid we saw nothing. Our trip was rather dull. The road was a little rough, and we were tired from the long travel through the Dark Forest, but we never saw anything. I only wish to get on our way so I can be with my grandmother before she passes."

Lord Parlimae smiled and said, "I haven't seen you since you were a child. Your family worked these lands for many years. I was sad to see you go. After your accident, I lost touch with your father but have monitored your progress. I was happy to hear of your marriage to the duke."

He paused, apology written on his face. "Unfortunately, I'm afraid the papers presented by Colonel Voelker are in order. We are delighted to have you, even if the circumstances are not ideal."

Mi Lady nodded graciously. She knew there was no point in arguing. If the king had made that decree, nobody would disobey. To do so was to risk the guillotine.

Lord Parlimae extended his hand toward the man seated to his right. "I'm sure you remember my son, William, as you played together as children. Someday he will be the lord of this castle. And he will have to deal with people like Colonel Voelker."

"Let's hope not any time soon, Father," William said with a smile as he bowed his head slightly to mi Lady. "It is good to see you again."

There was something strange about William. He hadn't said anything while Voelker was in the room, and he had a smug look on his face. I didn't like him. The way he addressed mi Lady seemed insincere. He was going along with the events of the day, but his demeanor suggested he had a hidden agenda.

William's features were more defined than his father's. His hair was jet black and very thick. His jaw and chin were chiseled, which made his sideways grin look edgy. His morning coat couldn't hide his broad chest and strong shoulders. I got the impression he knew how handsome he was, and he liked everyone else to know too.

"And to the right of William is the captain of my guard," said Lord Parlimae. "May I present Jonathan Barkslow."

Barkslow bowed his head slightly in greeting. He was a more serious man than William, not smug or full of himself. His bow wasn't just polite; it was respectful.

Although he was neat in appearance, his beard was a bit long. He was rough and unrefined, lean almost to the point of skinniness. He may not have been as big as William, but Barkslow gave the impression he could handle himself. I pegged him for a scrapper who had already survived the odds. He was clearly a dangerous man.

He didn't like Voelker telling us we couldn't leave either. But he was also a soldier and understood orders. When he read the parchment, I'd noticed a defiant look on his face, but he didn't argue.

It was clear we couldn't leave. There wasn't much we could do now, so we ate breakfast.

"I'm glad to hear your journey was uneventful," William said. "You must have gotten very lucky leaving Mercel when you did. The forest is known to be quite dangerous, especially at night. You didn't see any-thing unusual?"

His voice was laced with skepticism, but mi Lady paid it no mind. She looked up with a smile. "It is good to see you again too. It has been a long time. But I'm afraid, no, we didn't see anything. We weren't in Mercel but a moment."

She bowed slightly to Captain Barkslow. "It is my pleasure to make your acquaintance, Captain. I am disappointed at the circumstances. I guess we are fortunate you are both here. Surely there is no safer place in the region."

"Aside from ghost stories and great beasts of the forest, we've heard of some travelers encountering thieves in secluded areas. It was lucky you didn't run across them. Highwaymen can be a murderous and nasty group." William paused. "Night is an unusual time to travel."

"Indeed," mi Lady replied. "Traveling at night is a bit risky, but I need to get to Trevordeaux as soon as possible. Grandmother's illness has made it urgent. I haven't seen her since I married."

William smiled and nodded. He didn't press the subject, but I could see it in his eyes: he knew she was lying.

The look on her face said she didn't trust him either. It was painful to watch the two of them talk, each of them holding their true thoughts behind lies.

William pointed to the black wolf hanging on the wall behind his father. "I killed him many, many years ago. In the forest not far from here. It was a very intense hunt. He was a worthy adversary but no match for me." His voice was dark and grim as he spoke. "Wolves can be very large and dangerous in these parts. Most folks don't like hav-ing them around. They kill our livestock and sometimes threaten our people. Voelker is going to have his hands full if he encounters one like that."

William continued to boast about how he and a few friends had scoured the countryside hunting packs of wolves. They killed countless numbers and hung their pelts high on the castle walls for all to see.

Retaliation, he called it. Wolves had been killing the farmers' animals. The villagers had to stand watch over their herds just to make sure they didn't lose any animals overnight. Some of them had dogs to help, but dogs were no match for a pack of wolves.

A couple of the villagers had been hurt. One died, and they were all afraid. There had been a number of people killed on the road in the wild country. Rumors of these packs and mutilated deaths persisted.

It got so bad the villagers brought their herds inside the castle walls. This created a new set of problems, and it became clear the village needed a more-permanent solution. The villagers were fed up and demanded protection.

So Lord Parlimae decided to have William and a few others eradicate the wolves in the valley. They hunted and killed every wolf for miles. The land had been peaceful until now.

It was clear William enjoyed killing. His eyes lit up when he talked about hunting, and not just the wolves. He gloried in tales of how he killed the other animal mounts in the room. He recalled stories of old hunts as if he were reliving every moment. When talking about blood and gore, he relished the details, describing every last bit. And he got excited when narrating the moment of each animal's death.

I had been around hunters all my life. My father and uncles would go on hunting trips. They all came back with stories. But there was something deeper, disturbing about the way William described things.

After we finished eating, mi Lady stood up. As was polite custom, Lord Parlimae, William, and Captain Barkslow all rose. "Thank you for breakfast, my lord," she said. "I like to walk a bit after I eat, and I could use some air. If we must stay, I should like to look around, if that is acceptable."

"Whatever you need, my dear," said Lord Parlimae. "Please feel free to explore the castle. It has been some time since you were here. Much is the same, but I am sure much has changed. I would recommend staying within the walls. The drawbridge shall remain down for now, but if there is trouble, it will be raised. The back gate has been permanently closed. There is no other way into the castle."

Mi Lady smiled and walked out of the hall. I followed her to the courtyard outside. Several guards stood at the gate, keeping an eye on the road. Peasants moved around within the castle walls, doing various chores.

We made our way to the stables, and I stayed close by as we passed the barracks. Two of the Hessians leaned against the wall with their hats over their eyes. Another slept on a wooden bench. Colonel Voelker sat at a wooden table outside. He was looking over a map, consulting with one of his men. They lifted their heads to watch us walk by.

Mi Lady bowed her head to the colonel as a sign of acknowledgment and respect. The colonel leaned back in his seat. He did not return the nod.

The Hessian horses were in the front stalls. Mi Lady eyed the Hessian saddles but passed them by. She grabbed a couple of apples from a bucket beside the door, then made her way to Arca's stall. He and Killian were in a few stalls further down. The entire team had gotten plenty of rest and looked eager to get going. Arca bobbed his head when he saw her. He clearly liked her.

She stopped to give Killian an apple, and by the time she presented the second apple to Arca, his head was bobbing with impatience. She stroked his muzzle, then looked over at the carriage. "How long will it take you to harness the team?"

"Mi Lady, you want me to harness the team?"

"Not yet. I just want to know how long it would take." She looked back out the barn door. "We are not staying."

"What about the king's order, mi Lady?" I asked.

She looked at me with defiance in her eyes. "Is that a problem?"

"No. No, mademoiselle. Whenever you give the order, we will leave. I'm just not sure we can get past the guards, or the Hessians," I said.

"I don't trust the Hessians, and I suspect you don't either," she said. "Be ready. We might be stuck here for now, but when the opportunity presents itself, we're leaving."

"I'm with you, of course, mi Lady, but what about the black wolf and . . . the other thing?" I asked.

"We'll be okay. But we might not, if we stay here," she said.

# FIVE

# THE HESSIANS

*T*he sun had moved higher in the sky, and the day was bright and warm. I was sure the temperature would be cooler in the forest. The canopy of trees would prevent much of the sunlight from getting through, just as it had blocked the moonlight.

Following our conversation in the stable, mi Lady walked the inside perimeter of the castle. After that, she made her way inside to eat lunch with Lord Parlimae and William.

I decided to stay closer to the horses. There was a small market and butcher shop inside the castle walls, not far from the stable. A few of the peasant ladies working at the market invited me to eat with them. We sat outside the butcher's shop and watched the activity in the courtyard as we ate. Captain Barkslow made his rounds, stopping at each guard station. He must have informed them of the king's order because the number of guards securing the castle increased.

Someone must have notified the peasantry so they could find safety. A crowd of villagers was coming across the drawbridge now. Others guided animals to various buildings inside the walls.

When I finished eating with the ladies, I returned to the stables to prepare the harnesses. I wanted to be ready to flee at mi Lady's word. Harnessing four horses wasn't going to be easy on short notice, but if I arranged them in the right order, they'd be easier to grab in a hurry. I would get the horses lined up and buckle them to the carriage before anybody could stop me. The team was getting more restless by the hour, which would make getting them in line harder.

Colonel Voelker's voice startled me out of my thoughts. "It looks as if you are making preparations to leave."

"No. Keeping busy. Passing the time is all," I said, grabbing a brush to run over Arca's mane.

Voelker didn't react. He slowly walked around the carriage, inspecting every inch. "That's funny. The way you have those harnesses laid out, it looks like you are planning to leave, and in a hurry."

"What is it you want, Colonel?" I said coarsely. I wasn't intimidated by him any more than mi Lady was.

"Straight to the point. I like that," he said. "Why did you lie about being in the alley? You were just leaving when we arrived on the scene. You saw us give chase to the beasts through the busted fence. Yet you lied about being there. I shall like to know why."

"I didn't lie about anything. I never said I wasn't there. Nobody asked me, so I said nothing," I quipped. "The question was posed to mi Lady, and she wasn't there."

"Don't be clever. She was in the bar that night, just before the murders." He paused to look at my reaction. "Yes, I remembered you both being there."

I kept brushing Arca, and he continued to inspect the carriage. "Would you have me believe you didn't tell her about the gruesome scene in the alley? Or that nobody said a word? The entire village was terrified. And you drove this carriage from town right after, as quickly as you could. One of my men saw you racing out of town with her in the back."

He gave a long pause, but I refused to fill his silences with information about that night.

"Why did she lie?" he hissed impatiently. "Let me guess: she knows the beast, doesn't she?" He stopped his inspection, looking at me from the other side of the carriage. "It doesn't matter to me. I'm going to find that beast, and I'm going to kill it."

"This seems a bit personal for a bunch of wolves. Much more than a paid hunt," I said.

The colonel walked over to Killian and stroked his muzzle. Killian bobbed his head up and down—like me, he disliked Voelker. "I like this one. He has a great deal of fire in him. Reminds me of a horse I once knew."

The colonel kept petting Killian, undeterred by Killian's protest. "Do you know what I am? What we are?" he asked.

"Hessians," I answered.

"That is correct. Many years ago, I served under a great commander. We left our homeland and traveled to the Americas to fight alongside the British Crown. They hired us to aid their army in a war with ceding colonists.

"There were fifty men in my regiment. I was but a frontline soldier then. But my commander was a great man, a seasoned fighter. He had survived many battles over the years—wars with the Rus, the British, and many others.

"It was fall, much like it is now. The days were often cool, but they warmed when the sun was high. The evenings and nights were cold.

"We fought mostly in forests—not unlike this one, although the Dark Forest is a bit thicker. But there was a section of forest in the upper lands of the Americas that was thick and dark like this. Pines and big timber covered a long valley, or hollow. Not much light shined there. Nights seemed especially cold, and the entire place had a slower pace.

"Our army had marched through the dense forest, and the commander decided we should make camp in this hollow. We planned to make our way through the forest the next day.

"We built fires for our meals and warmth. They grew dim and we grew tired. Just as we were about to fall asleep, we heard the howl of wolves in the distance. It was nothing we hadn't heard before. We have wolves in our homeland, just like everywhere else in the world.

"But these howls were somehow different. The men weren't too concerned until the howls got closer. The howls became yips and barks, as if the wolves were talking to one another while they watched us.

"At first, it wasn't a problem. They were just sounds, and we had guards posted throughout the night. But the men started to grow concerned. We all knew the tales of the witches in that land, especially in Salem. They were the spawn of Satan, casting spells and placing curses on men. Sometimes those curses changed men into hideous beasts.

"As the sounds went on, anxiety got worse in the camp. The commander ordered extra men on the perimeter to watch over us. He told them to warn us if anything got close. Sometimes I think they were lucky to go first.

"In the middle of the night, when the moon was highest, we heard a scream. We all jumped to the ready, but our haste did not matter. The next man guarding the perimeter was snatched. His screams lasted a long time before the night fell silent. Then one by one, something dragged the men who stood watch into the darkness.

"None of us got any sleep that night. We turned our backs to the fires, ready for an attack. But none came. When dawn arrived, the forest was quiet—no howling, no sounds, not even the songs of the morning birds.

"Daylight broke through the cloudy skies and thick branches above as we packed up our gear. The commander sent a small group of scouts to find our lost men. They found no signs of the men. No traces. No blood. No tracks. Nothing.

"So we marched through the hollow, all of us suffering from a lack of sleep. We felt safe because it was the day. We were wrong. The howling started again when we reached the darkest part of the hollow. We came to a long, rough bridge. It was narrow and would only take a few horses and men at a time. We couldn't go around it—the land was too steep and there were logs everywhere. The only way ahead was over the bridge.

"Twilight was coming, and we needed to get across so we could make camp before the sun went down. Ten men started, entering beneath vines and tree limbs. With the overarching vegetation, the bridge looked like a cave, so dark we could barely see the other side. Two unlit torches stood at the entrance, but it was daylight, so nobody thought to light them.

"After the last man had disappeared beyond the day's light, the screaming began. All we could see were flashes from their muskets, one right after the other. In those flares of light, we saw the monster attacking them: a large, black creature with long fangs and claws. It struck at the men wildly, killing them one and then the next. In a matter of moments, there were no more musket flashes. The screams had stopped.

"Those of us waiting to cross aimed our muskets at the bridge, preparing to fire. But in a fit of rage, our commander drew his sword and charged his horse into the blackness. We could not fire, and we could not see.

"We heard him fighting the great beast. His horse stamping and letting out whinnies. Snarls and the snapping of teeth and sounds of a great struggle. Then everything went quiet.

"The lasting silence intensified our fear. Suddenly, we heard a *thump, thump, thump.* The commander's head had rolled out from the darkness and landed at our feet.

"Terrified, we all instinctively fired into the black. Ten men unloaded their muskets into the pitch blackness with one purpose: to kill the creature. When the smoke cleared from our guns, we reloaded and fired again. Two men lit the torches, and after reloading, we followed them inside. The beast was nowhere to be found. The torchlight revealed the horror. The soldiers, our men, had been savagely killed—torn to pieces from stem to stern. Our commander's headless corpse lay right in the middle."

The colonel touched the saber at his side. "This is the sword my commander used to attack the beast. It is all that is left of that great man." He paused. "I have only seen bodies killed like that one other time. In that alley at Mercel."

He leaned in toward me, and his tone turned to hatred. "Trust me when I tell you, I am going to kill that creature. I'm going to cut off its head with this very sword. And I'll kill anyone who gets in my way."

Colonel Voelker turned and walked out of the stables. I stood there for a moment, taking in everything he had said. Putting the brush down, I walked to the entrance of the stable and watched Voelker as he joined his men at the barracks.

The creature that saved us wasn't Voelker's beast. The colonel had seen that monster a long time ago and in a continent far away. But that didn't matter to Voelker or his men. He wasn't going to stop until he killed all of its kind.

While Voelker was busy with his men, I needed to find mi Lady. She needed to know that Voelker was aware of her lies. And she needed to know why he was so determined to hunt down the creature.

I scoured the castle grounds for sight of her. I saw William at the armory, where he was talking to a guard and inspecting weapons. Barkslow wasn't around, but I passed his men everywhere. As for mi Lady, she was neither inside the castle nor within the courtyard. It wasn't likely she would have wandered outside the walls.

Then it occurred to me where she might be. There was one place I had not looked.

When we first arrived at the castle, the servants had taken me to my room in the tower by way of a tall staircase. We'd passed a set of large wooden doors in the foyer, across from the dining hall. There had been a cross carved into them. They must have led to the chapel.

I ran through the foyer and opened one of the chapel doors. As I had suspected, mi Lady was kneeling at the altar.

A large wooden cross hung high above. Stained glass windows allowed daylight to enter in an array of colors, which shone on the cross. Flickering flames filled the space with even more light. Some candles sat in rows at the front of the chapel and on nearby tables;

others lined the walls on either side of the pews. Parishioners entering to worship could light a candle in prayer.

Mi Lady was in the front row with her hood up. Without turning to look at me, she asked, "Is everything ready?"

I moved closer to her before I replied. The room was large, and the ceilings were high. Sound carried through the chamber. Her question had set off a loud echo. It'd be easy for an eavesdropper to overhear, and I wasn't sure if anyone was nearby.

"Yes, Duchess," I said softly. "Everything is in order."

"Don't call me that." She didn't say it angrily, but she was firm.

"Yes, your grace." I said, bowing slightly.

"Don't call me that either," she said without looking.

"How should I address you then?" I asked.

"Mi Lady is fine," she said, looking back at me. "I've grown accustomed to how you say it anyway." Then she looked back at the altar. "What time is it?" She had been in prayer awhile, and it seemed she did not know the lateness of the hour.

"It is late in the day. There are only a few hours left before the sun goes down. I would suspect the evening meal draws close," I said.

She arose from her kneeling position and backed up to sit in the first pew. Her eyes were still fixed on the cross. I walked up and sat beside her. Her face was sad, pensive.

"Mi Lady," I said, "The Hessians are determined to kill the beast. It is more than a job to the colonel. It is a personal mission. A vendetta."

"He knows . . . the creature?" she asked.

"No, mi Lady. I don't think so. He and his men fought something in the Americas years ago. I think he just hates them," I answered. "There is something else, mi Lady. He knows you lied about being in Mercel when those people were killed. He is convinced you know the beast."

She looked over at me for a moment and then returned her gaze to the cross. "It doesn't matter. I have to get to Trevordeaux. My grandmother needs me." She lowered her head sadly and said softly, "I will need you when the time comes."

"The colonel is not going to just let us leave," I said.

Eyes fixed to the cross, she said, "Let me worry about him. There will be an opportunity. Make sure the horses are ready. If we can get through the valley, we will be all right."

"Yes, mi Lady," I said as I stood. I bowed in respect to her, knelt at the end of the pew, and made the sign of the cross. I opened the chapel door just as a servant came in.

"Lord Parlimae has asked me to inform you that supper is served in the main dining hall, mi Lady," the servant announced.

She stood up and smiled at him, making her way to the door. I held it open for her, then followed her and the servant out of the chapel and through the foyer. When she turned toward the dining hall, I continued to the front doors. She stopped and called out to me as I was leaving. "Are you not joining us for supper?"

"No thank you, mi Lady. I'm going to get the horses some grain. I still have food left over from lunch. You know where to find me if you need me," I said as I exited through the castle doors.

Outside the barracks, the Hessians were eating supper with some of the castle guards. They all appeared to be getting along nicely. Seemed odd to me, as Hessians were generally the enemy of the French. Then again, it was odd for the king to hire them in the first place.

King Louis must have been pretty desperate to hire Hessian mercenaries to kill wolves in his land. Either that, or these men had left the Hessian army and were acting completely on their own.

The peasantry didn't seem to mind the Hessians being there. They moved about the castle grounds beneath the low-hanging sun, finishing their work for the day. Some moved goods to storage buildings, while others tended livestock.

As I was about to enter the stable, an alarm bell rang over the castle grounds. The barracks became alive with activity. Castle guards ran toward the drawbridge. The colonel ordered his men to stay put while he and his captain ran to the gate. Everywhere I looked, people were frantically running around.

I raced past the barracks on my way to the drawbridge, weaving my way through the small crowd that had formed. Whatever the commotion, I wanted to get a first accounting of it.

The drawbridge was still down, and a crowd had gathered around a cart. A couple of villagers had pulled it across the bridge and into the castle courtyard. Guards on the high walls remained at their posts but strained to see what had happened. I inched closer to get a look too.

A farmer lay in the back of the cart, his leg injured and losing a lot of blood. Writhing in pain, he spoke feverishly about something that had attacked him in the field. He had found one of his sheep torn apart, the sight of which caused the panicked herd to flee deeper into the valley. He ran to investigate.

He'd been running back to the village when the beast jumped out of the woods, caught him, and tore open his leg. A few other farmers witnessed the attack and grabbed their muskets, but the creature ran off before anyone could fire.

The castle physician shoved his way through the crowd. He cinched large pieces of cloth around the man's leg to put pressure on the wound and stop the bleeding. But the gashes were deep, and the victim had already lost a lot of blood.

Colonel Voelker and his captain pushed through the crowd, and I followed on their heels. "Describe the beast!"

The farmer could barely speak now. The loss of blood and severity of his wounds had taken their toll. He tried to repeat the story but passed out. He was just barely alive. The physician ordered a group of men to take the farmer to the back of the castle, where he kept quarters. They pulled the cart away as Lord Parlimae, William, and mi Lady ran out of the castle.

"What has happened?" demanded Lord Parlimae.

One of the farmers who had saved the injured man repeated the story. He turned to the colonel. "It was hard to see the animal that did this, what with the setting sun and the shadows from the trees."

He swallowed and continued. "It was dark. Something jumped out of the woods—a huge, monstrous thing with long, black claws. When we raised our muskets, the beast let out a hideous howl or scream. I've never heard anything like that." The man swallowed hard again. "That was no wolf. I can tell you that."

Without another word, Colonel Voelker ran back to the barracks. He and the other Hessians grabbed their gear and scurried to the livery. Within minutes, a stampede of horses pounded out of the stables, their riders ready for battle.

They rode up to the crowd, skidding to a stop in front of Lord Parlimae. The colonel's voice rang out over the courtyard. "Get everyone in the castle! No one is to leave until we return. We will take care of the beast this night!"

Voelker turned his horse toward the gate and used the reins to whip its haunch. The palomino reared upward, and with powerful back legs, sprung forward. It hit the ground in full gallop. He whipped the reins back and forth across the horse's back to increase its speed. His men all kicked their horses into action and followed him out of the castle. The horses' hooves thundered across the drawbridge and kicked up a plume of dust. Moments later, they slipped out of sight.

Lord Parlimae ordered the guards to sound the bell that would draw the villagers inside the castle walls. Several guards waited at the drawbridge. The moment everyone was inside, they'd raise the bridge. Guards on the walls readied their muskets. Others ran to the armory for more weapons and ammunition.

Mi Lady calmly walked over to me, leaned in, and spoke softly. "We have to get out of here before that drawbridge rises."

# SIX

# NEAR DEATH

*I* ran to the stables as fast as my legs would carry me. As long as the bells were ringing, I would have time to flee. They wouldn't stop until every villager was inside the castle walls.

Buckling in the second-row horses was easy. The carriage faced the right direction, and having the harnesses laid out in the correct order sped up the process. One by one, I hooked them in their proper place on the doubletree.

Killian and Arca were agitated. They could feel the energy in the castle, and the frantic sound of the bells added to their tension. Killian was so excited he reared up when I pulled him out of the stall. I almost lost my grip on the rein, but a strong hand landed above mine and helped me pull him down.

I turned to find William. He'd entered the stables when my back was turned and was now helping me get the horses in line. As he strapped in Killian, I grabbed Arca and pulled him in place. He was easier to coax than Killian, amped up but old enough to know how to control himself.

Once they were in place, William jumped onto the seat with me. "Let's go!"

I released the brake, snapped the reins, and hurried the carriage out of the stables. We roared up to the doors of the castle, stopping at the base of the steps. The guards gave us startled looks as we approached.

Mi Lady saw us coming and moved to the side. When we stopped, she jumped into the carriage and slid the window open.

Lord Parlimae grabbed Killian's halter, trying to prevent us from leaving. "William, what are you doing? Mademoiselle, you cannot leave. It's the king's orders."

There was genuine fear in his eyes. William jumped down, grabbing Lord Parlimae by the arms and pulling him aside. I still hadn't determined why William was helping us leave.

"At the crossroads," William yelled to me without taking his eyes off mi Lady, "near the forest edge, continue southeast. This will take you back toward the sea at the other end of the forest. From there, you won't be far from Port Calibre. It's a good place to rest the horses before Trevordeaux."

"William, no!" Lord Parlimae pleaded.

"Safe travels, mi Lady. I'm sure we'll see each other again very soon."

Something about the way he'd said *soon* sent a shiver down my spine. His tone had been ominous. I looked into his eyes. He was helping us leave, but I was hoping to never see him again.

The crowd was no longer blocking the path to the drawbridge, so we could make a speedy exit. I cracked the reins, barking out commands to Arca and Killian. The team pulled hard, picking up speed. We crossed the drawbridge quickly and loudly. I steered them down the road, clouds of dust accompanying us through the village.

The houses were all boarded up. Windows were secured with shutters, and the streets were vacant. The peasants had all made it inside the castle. It was an eerie feeling to go through a town without any people.

I looked back at the castle as the drawbridge was rising. It closed with a loud bang. Nothing would be getting in or coming out.

We made our way through the village quickly. When we reached the crossroad, I steered southeast, just as William suggested. The road ran down the middle of long, open fields. The farmers' crops appeared near harvest, some growing high on each side of the road.

A light headwind came our way. I stayed alert but didn't see another soul. No Hessians. No wolves. No beasts.

We approached the forest as the sun was just about to fall below the horizon. Only a few minutes of daylight remained. I pulled the reins to slow the team. There didn't seem to be a need for an all-out run. Arca, Killian, and the rest of the horses were winded from the sprint out of the castle, but they were well rested from their time in the stables.

The sun finally went down, but luckily the sky was clear and the moon shone brightly. I had vowed not to travel at night again on this trip, but there didn't seem to be any way to avoid it. At least everything had gone smoothly so far.

There was no sign of trouble, so I slowed the team to a stop and hopped down. Mi Lady watched as I lit each of the carriage lamps. The moon may have been bright, but I knew how dark the road through the forest could get.

When I was finished, I jumped back into the driver's seat and started the team again. Arca and Killian didn't need much guidance, so I started to relax. The sounds of the night put me at ease.

The road in this part of the forest was a lot wider than the section that ran from mi Lady's mansion to Mercel. There were few turns and no side roads, so I let the road guide the horses forward.

I began thinking of my family, wondering what they were doing. My mother would be finishing her chores for the day, cleaning up after supper and preparing for tomorrow's breakfast. My father would be completing some little project before he retired for the evening. And my little brother would be looking after the animals one more time before bed, making sure they were safe for the night.

I imagined what tomorrow might hold for them and could almost smell my mother's fresh bread. She would bake it in the morning and place it on the windowsill to cool. If she had leftover dough, she would make little round buns. If I were home, I would steal a few as I walked by.

For the first time in a long time, I missed home. It had been a while since I saw my family. I resided at the stable company but had paid them a visit before taking on this job. That was a few weeks ago.

I'd left to pick up this new carriage. It had come on a ship, crafted in a faraway land and ordered specially for this trip. The company would make enough money from this job to purchase this ride and use it to bolster future profits later.

After retrieving the carriage, I went straight to pick up mi Lady. It took me nearly a week to make it to her house. The ride there was pleasant, but it made for a long trip.

My father always teased me about wanting adventure. He would say no moss ever grew under my feet. He didn't like that I went away, but he understood and respected the need to earn a living.

Thinking about home was a good distraction from thoughts of our journey. The previous night had been long and rough. The circumstances were disturbing to relive. It seemed like a dream or nightmare.

But that was behind us now, in more ways than one. Tonight seemed brighter, and not just because this stretch of trees let more moonlight through. The forest was no longer scary, and the smell in the air was fresh.

The Hessians had ordered us to stay, but just as mi Lady said, once we got out of the valley, we would be okay. There was no sign of the mercenaries. They must have gone the other way. For all I knew, they'd already killed those wolves. I just hoped they did us all a favor and killed the black one.

We had been traveling for quite some time when the route cut between two large hills. The road was wide and flat, making it easier to see despite the forest surroundings.

I twisted to the side to peek into the coach. Mi Lady was looking out the window, a look of contentment or relief on her face. I was sure she was anxious to be with her grandmother, but the events of this trip had to be on her mind.

When I turned back around, the road was curving around the hill. The forest thinned, revealing a field of tall grass that extended to the forest. We rode with the field on one side and a large body of water on the other. The smell of salt filled the air. It was a good, clean odor.

Sparse tufts of tall grasses intermingled with mounds of sand. The surf once encroached here but had since receded, leaving behind a moonlike landscape. We went along for some distance before mi Lady opened her window and yelled, "Driver! Could you stop for a moment please?"

I pulled the team to a halt next to a beach. The surf was coming in with high waves crashing onto the shore. Foam settled in large tide pools.

Wind hurried across the water, urging white-capped waves to roll. They struck rocks and sand in a soothing rhythm. It was quite a site under the moonlight.

The carriage door opened before I could hop down. Mi Lady stepped out and walked toward the surf with bare feet, letting the sand squish between her toes. A look of deep thought crossed her brow as she watched the ebb and flow of the water.

I was standing beside Arca when that strange feeling came over me again. I looked down the shore to mi Lady. She seemed fine, but the air became heavy. Something had changed.

Arca let out a puff of breath and shuffled his feet. Killian started to fidget, as did the second-row horses. Their uneasiness only grew.

I could read the horses, and I knew that feeling. "MI LADY!" I yelled. "I THINK WE SHOULD BE GOING—RATHER QUICKLY, I'M AFRAID!"

My senses were honed. Something wicked was here.

I didn't want to make any sudden movements. Cautiously, I made my way toward the driver's seat to get my musket. After the other night, I knew the gun might not protect us, but it was the only weapon I had. Mi Lady had walked a good distance from the carriage. Hopefully, I would be able to hit anything that came near her.

I continued to move slowly past the horses. After a few steps, I stopped and scanned the forest. I thought I saw movement in the tall grass, but it may have been shadows or the wind. I almost moved on, almost continued to the beach, but then I saw them.

Some of the shadows were darker than others. They seemed to have a distinct shape. I squinted at the tall grass, catching a glimpse of amber eyes.

My heart beat so loud I could barely hear anything else. My knees trembled. I could barely see the creatures, and I was already terrified.

I looked to mi Lady, who was slowly making her way back to the carriage. She was across the beach, too far to have noticed anything. There was a strong breeze coming off the water. Between that and the sound of the waves, she would have trouble hearing any warning I gave.

I tried to remain calm. If I made any sudden movements, I might trigger an attack. Maybe she would make it to the carriage before they struck.

When my gaze returned to the tall grass, it collided with a set of steady eyes. All around, amber eyes flashed in the dark, disappearing and reappearing again and again. The wolves were moving, getting into a better position. But the eyes closest to me continued to stare.

As I slowly reached for my musket, I heard a low growl coming from behind the carriage. A warning. I froze in place. I was scared to move, but I had to look.

I glanced out the corner of my eye but couldn't spot the animal. I steeled myself and slowly turned my head toward the sound. At the edge of the grass, beyond the shadows, stood a black wolf!

It was the same large male we'd crossed on the road from Mercel—I was sure of it. An overextended snarl showed his long, white teeth. The sides of his mouth dripped with saliva. A long string stretched from his jaw to a puddle on the ground.

Slowly, he took two steps toward me. Another growl rumbled in his chest. This time, the sound was louder, deeper, longer, and more menacing. He seemed to be saying, "I got you now."

I had one foot up on the step of the carriage. The musket was just beyond my grasp. If I could reach it, I might be able to get a shot off. But he was so close to me now. If I made one mistake, he would be on me.

Without turning my head, I slid my eyes to the beach. Mi Lady had stopped about halfway to the carriage, a look of terror on her face. Her gaze didn't stray from the hulking form of the black wolf.

Something rustled in the field, and out of the corner of my eye, I saw shadows advancing from the grass. The remainder of the pack was creeping toward me. It was hard to tell how many there were.

When the black wolf turned his gaze to the pack, I saw my chance. I scrambled into the driver's seat, barely reaching it before he pounced. I vaulted across the seat, landing on the other side of the carriage. I tried to grab the musket as I went, but my fingers fumbled. There was no time to stop for it. If I hesitated, he would reach me.

His jaws snapped, the hideous sound of clacking teeth ringing in the air. His bite missed my leg, and the motion sent his head bouncing off the side of the carriage. The impact tumbled him to the ground.

Gathering himself, he made a second leap onto the seat. The horses went wild. Arca and Killian reared up and then slammed down, lunging in an attempt to escape. The carriage brake kept the wheels from turning, but the force of the horses' movements jumped the carriage ahead. This jolted the black wolf, causing him to stumble in the driver's seat. The distraction was just enough for me to race inside the carriage.

The rest of the wolf pack attacked the carriage, snarling and showing their teeth. The black wolf came after me just as I shut the door. He snarled and scratched in a fit of rage.

My nightmare was coming true. These were not ordinary wolves. It was obvious the pack wasn't interested in the horses. They were here to kill *us*!

The doors and windows on the carriage were not going to hold them back. It wouldn't be long before they broke through the glass, ripped the carriage apart, and had at me. As that thought slashed through my mind, the black wolf retreated. I looked at the pack that had surrounded the carriage. The wolves fell back.

The black wolf shifted his attention to the beach. The rest of the wolves followed suit. Their eyes now fixated on mi Lady. She had not moved since the attack began. Out there on the beach, there was no place for her to run.

The pack crept to the back of the carriage. Their eyes never drifted from mi Lady. She looked at each of them, then made her move. She picked up her dress and ran down the beach in the opposite direction, her cape flowing dramatically behind her.

The wolves didn't move right away. They stared at one another, as if surprised she'd chosen to run. They released excited howls. The black wolf was the first to move. The others sprinted after him across the sand. They formed an inverted V behind her, the black wolf in the lead.

Their brief pause before bolting provided her a chance at escape. But it wasn't going to be enough. There wasn't anywhere for her to go. The wolves weren't running at full speed, and they were still going to catch her easily.

I could only watch in horror as they caught up. I rushed out of the carriage and climbed into the driver's seat. Grabbing my musket, I swung it to my shoulder and took aim.

I couldn't fire. They were too far away. If I missed, I could accidentally shoot mi Lady.

The black wolf slowed his pace, and the others matched his speed. When they got closer, they fanned out around her to prevent her from darting in any direction but forward. They were dogs herding a lost sheep toward their hungry mouths.

With no clear shot from my perch, I jumped down and ran toward them. I spotted some large rocks ahead of her. Those could provide cover if she could reach them in time. If I were closer, I could fire a shot or two to distract the wolves and give her time to flee. I ran a little faster to get near the pack.

Then the unthinkable happened. As mi Lady was running, she looked over her shoulder. A second later, she stumbled to the ground. The air left my lungs as I watched the wolves descend upon her.

They howled excitedly, surrounding her crumpled form. They could sense the kill. She turned on her side as they closed in. The black wolf attacked first, leaping high into the air before diving at her with open jaws. The impact caused her head to snap back, and it hit a rock with a loud crack.

I worried for a moment that the strike had knocked her unconscious, but she shifted in the sand. She raised her arm to defend herself, but the black wolf's teeth tore into her flesh. A second wolf grabbed her leg and shook it violently. She cried out in terror and screamed for help.

As the two wolves continued their assault, the rest of the pack paced in a semicircle. They howled and yipped excitedly, sensing she was about to be finished off.

Tears flowed from my eyes as I ran. I came to a sliding stop in the sand and raised the musket to my shoulder. Maybe I could take out one of those evil bastards before they tore her apart.

Just as I was about to pull the trigger, a masked man thundered from the tree line on the back of a buckskin! He was hunkered down in the saddle and whipping the horse furiously to go faster. The horse's hooves tossed sand high in the air as it gained speed. It cut a straight path toward the wolfpack!

When he was close enough, the rider pulled a musket from a sling. In one fluid motion, he dropped the reins, moved the musket to his shoulder, took aim, and fired. The shot rang out with a loud bang.

The musket ball ripped across the black wolf's face. Blood, flesh, and fur went flying. The force of the bullet caused his head to turn violently to the side.

Reloading would've taken too long, so the rider quickly secured the musket and pulled a pistol from his waist. Wasting no time, he fired a second shot! This bullet struck the black wolf in the neck. The wolf went limp, instantly falling to the ground. I raised my musket high above my head and yelled in triumph. "YEAAAAAHHH!"

The rider pulled yet another pistol from his waist and fired at the wolf that was tearing at mi Lady's leg. When the bullet struck, the wolf let out a yelp and let go of her leg. It scrambled away, pushing through the pack, which still circled mi Lady. They watched the wounded wolf run in the opposite direction.

Then, unexpectedly, the black wolf leapt to his feet. My mouth dropped open—I'd been sure the shot to the neck had killed him. The black wolf leaned forward, growling at the rider. He raised his head and let out a hideous roar.

As the sound filled the air, the other wolves retreated. They darted across the beach and toward the field, taking the shortest route back to the forest. Each looked back at the rider while running, seemingly afraid of pursuit.

They disappeared into the tall grass, swaying the blades as they ran through. Within moments, they were across the field and entering the woods without a trace.

Bleeding and in great pain, mi Lady dragged herself onto the nearby rocks. The black wolf spared her a quick look before turning back to the rider, who was nearly upon him. Teeth bared and hackles on end, he snarled at the rider one last time before he ran.

The black wolf gave me wide berth as he raced by. He continued past the carriage and across the road, disappearing into the tall grass like the rest of the pack.

The rider pulled the buckskin to a stop in front of mi Lady, sending sand flying. He hopped down, secured his pistols, and ran over to her. She was badly injured and bleeding. Using the scarf from his neck, he wrapped her arm tightly where the black wolf's teeth had sharply dug in. He pulled the black mask from his face and used it to wrap her leg.

I ran toward them. As I got closer, I recognized him as the stranger from the tavern in Mercel. His clothes were a little different—tonight he wore a black tricorne and a blue woodland coat—but he otherwise looked the same.

When he finished dressing her leg, he turned to the wound on the back of her head. He ripped cloth from his shirt and used it to stop the bleeding. He tore another piece of cloth and wrapped it around her head to keep the bandage in place.

Blood from her wounds seeped through his wrappings. The bandages were not enough to stop the bleeding. He picked her up and carried her to his horse. With mi Lady in his arms, he mounted the buckskin. The stranger looked back at me and then, without a word, rode off.

"HEY! WAIT! WHERE ARE YOU GOING?" I yelled.

He never looked back. A swift kick to the horse's sides, and within moments they disappeared over the mounds of sand. Over the sound of the wind and the waves, I heard horse hooves galloping down the road.

I ran back to the carriage, jumped into the driver's seat, kicked the brake free, and snapped the reins hard to the left. Arca and Killian pulled hard. It was difficult to turn four horses and a large carriage, and I only hoped we weren't taking too long. We needed to quickly ride in the direction he'd taken mi Lady if we had any chance of catching up.

As soon as we faced the right direction, I ran the carriage hard. We crossed from the field through the trees, and I had to slow slightly. There was still plenty of moonlight for traveling, but the forest was just dark enough to make it hard to see the road.

We trotted along for a while, but the trail went cold. There were no obvious tracks, no signs the stranger had come this way at all. It didn't help that it was still night. Somewhere along the way, he must have jumped off the road and entered the forest.

Frustrated, I pulled the reins and stopped. Now what was I going to do? I had to find her, but I didn't know where to begin. I had no idea who this stranger was or where he was from. He might've been a highwayman or road agent—he dressed like one—but it was hard to tell.

One thing I knew for sure: he was the stranger at the pub. The innkeeper had seemed familiar with him. I would have to return to Mercel and see if anybody knew him. I really didn't want to go back. It would mean risking another encounter with the wolves, and I had no desire to tangle with the black wolf again. But I had no other choice. I couldn't just leave her.

As much as I wanted to find her quickly, I needed help. I set off for Castle Parlimae. I wasn't very anxious to go there either. After all, we did violate the king's orders. I wasn't sure how Lord Parlimae would receive me, especially now that I'd lost the Duchess of Harcourt. But Lord Parlimae was clearly fond of mi Lady. I just hoped they didn't arrest me upon my return.

By the time I reached the castle, evening had fallen upon the land. The ocean must have been further away than I realized last night. Life filled the valley again. Peasants had returned to their homes. And the great drawbridge was down.

I thundered across the drawbridge, and it occurred to me the Hessians may have returned. Perhaps they caught the black wolf and his pack after our attack. That would solve one problem, but it wouldn't help me find mi Lady.

I pulled up to the front of the castle and yanked the brake. As I jumped down, Captain Barkslow came out of the barracks. Several servants ran in my direction. Lord Parlimae strode out the castle. There was no sign of William, and there didn't appear to be as many guards on duty.

Lord Parlimae peered in the coach. He could see it was empty. "What's wrong, child? Where is—"

"We were attacked by a pack of wolves about half a day's ride from here, on a beach near a sea," I said, cutting him off before he could ask about mi Lady. "A masked rider came along and saved mi Lady from the wolves, but he took her."

"What? What do you mean he took her?" asked Barkslow.

"A blond man on a buckskin thundered in and shot one of the wolves. The others ran. He was bandaging her wounds, but she wouldn't stop bleeding. Before I could reach her, he picked her up, got on his horse, and rode off. I tried to find them, but I couldn't," I said frantically.

"How bad was she injured?" asked Lord Parlimae.

"I'm not sure," I said.

"Calm down, child. Did you recognize the rider?"

"Yes," I said. "I think so. I saw him in Mercel. He was in the tavern when mi Lady and I were there, just before we came here."

Lord Parlimae looked at Barkslow, who looked questioningly at me. His voice snapped with annoyance. "If he was wearing a mask, how did you recognize him?"

"He took off the mask and used it to bandage her leg. That's when I saw his face," I answered.

"What were you doing by the sea?" Lord Parlimae asked.

"We stopped near the shore to give the horses a rest. She got out of the carriage to walk the beach. That's when the wolves attacked. Two of them bit into her. The rider shot them, and the others ran," I said.

Annoyance pinched Lord Parlimae's brow and tightened his lips. "Yesterday, you said you didn't see a thing in Mercel."

Lord Parlimae and Barkslow looked at each other. They were clearly angry that mi Lady hadn't told them about Mercel. There wasn't anything I could do about that now.

"She never saw the murders," I said. "I saw the bodies in the alley. We left, fearing it was too dangerous to stay. I don't know why mi Lady didn't share that with you. Maybe she didn't want you to be angry that we stopped so late. Maybe she just didn't want to be caught up in the drama at Mercel. Or maybe she didn't want the Hessians to know."

Lord Parlimae just nodded. Barkslow's tone softened a little. "Tell me what happened in Mercel. What did you see that would cause you to leave in the middle of the night, to travel a dangerous countryside without an armed escort?"

"When we arrived at Mercel," I began, "we checked into our rooms at the inn. I boarded the horses and went to the tavern to get some supper. I ordered my ale, and as I sipped it, I noticed mi Lady at one of the tables.

"The Hessians were there, gambling in the back. A stranger came in—a tall, blond man wearing nice clothes. He ordered a drink and left. She left right after the stranger. I got nervous and went to look for her. The street was empty, so I checked her room. I thought she went inside."

"What do you mean you thought she went inside? Did she or did she not go back to her room?" Barkslow asked impatiently.

"I thought I saw her enter her room," I said. "I went to sleep but was awakened by some screams outside. The innkeeper banged at my door, going on about two people viciously attacked in the alley. We went outside, joining the rest of the pub's patrons where they clustered in the alley. I saw a man and a woman completely torn apart. The Hessians came to the alley and chased after the . . . whatever did that. I went back to mi Lady's room, but she wasn't there. I found her in the stables with the horses. We got the hell out of Mercel as quickly as we could and came straight here."

Barkslow shared a look with Lord Parlimae and then turned his skeptical gaze at me. His voice was angry as he spoke. "Is there anything else? Anything you're leaving out?"

Something told me to leave out our attack on the road from Mercel. It would be pretty hard to explain how we escaped that one. I knew better than to tell them about the wolf-man who defeated an angry pack of wolves and then shoved a giant tree aside. That would just seem crazy. If they didn't believe me, they might assume I made up the whole story.

I shook my head. "That's it. I swear. I came back here to ask for your help. Do you know anything about the man who took mi Lady?"

Barkslow leaned back, deep in thought. He regarded Lord Parlimae, asking a silent question with a quirk of his brow. Lord Parlimae nodded.

Barkslow ran back to the castle, barking orders to the servants who had been listening. They all dispersed and rushed about.

Lord Parlimae put his arm around me as he spoke. "Come inside, child, and warm up. We'll find her."

I pulled back. "Thank you, but I must go with them. I can't just sit here and not look for her."

"They're not leaving until the morning, child. It's far too dangerous to go now. The sun will be setting soon, and the country is too wild," Lord Parlimae said.

"I must leave for Mercel. If I start now, I can be there just after dark," I said as I ran back to my team and climbed into the driver's seat.

Just then, Barkslow came out of the castle. He was carrying a couple of muskets and some provisions under his arms. He looked at me as he hustled by and said, "We leave at first light."

"I'm leaving now," I said. "I'll meet you back here at noon tomorrow."

Barkslow stopped and shook his head slowly. "I know you wish to find her. I will help you, but you can't do her any good if you are killed. The woods are too dangerous right now. You and your horses will be killed. Please, stay the night, and I promise tomorrow morning we will go together. We are already preparing."

Lord Parlimae extended his hand. "Come, child. Captain Barkslow is right. It's at least half a day's ride to Mercel. You would be riding well into the night. We will find her. I have known her since she was a small child. I am afraid for her too. But she is resourceful, a fighter. She'll be all right. Besides, if this man wanted to harm her, he wouldn't have bandaged her wounds."

I stared at Arca and Killian as I thought. Lord Parlimae and Barkslow were right. I was kidding myself if I thought I could get there before nightfall. It would be very late by the time I reached Mercel. Getting myself and the horses killed would not help her. I didn't like it, but I was staying.

# SEVEN

# FEAR

$\mathcal{M}$y sleep was the restless sort. Even asleep, my mind was trying to make sense of everything that had happened since I met mi Lady. The events of the past two nights chased me out of sleep, and I lay still and quiet, trying to piece together the puzzle.

Blue eyes followed us through the forest. A brown wolf calmly watched us from the road near the meadow. Two people had been murdered in Mercel. And a pack of wolves attacked us twice, ignoring the horses as if they were on a mission to kill me and mi Lady. What was going on?

There was something amiss here too. Lord Parlimae was kind and generous, but his son, William, seemed as evil and creepy as anybody I'd ever met. And why did this castle need a captain of the guard? William had made it clear he was capable of defending against attack when he boasted about killing that wolf.

The Hessians were another issue. Colonel Voelker had made his personal vendetta clear, his determination and ruthless manner on full display. But I couldn't figure out why the king had hired them to rid the countryside of wolves. Usually, they fought for enemies of France, yet here they were as allies.

And now this damned stranger had reappeared. Mi Lady seemed to know him, but she refused to reveal, well, a lot. Even so, my mind drew a logical conclusion: the stranger, the brown wolf, and the beast were one and the same.

They had the same blue eyes and strange markings. I could only assume he'd visited us in a different form throughout the journey: protecting us as a wolf along the way and saving us from the black wolf's attack as a monstrous beast. Now, I realized, a werewolf.

And, of course, he'd appeared last night as a masked rider to save us from a second wolf attack. He had patched up mi Lady like some type of hero, then took off with her like a kidnapper. How was I supposed to know which he truly was?

If he was really the werewolf, why hadn't he transformed and killed the pack? Why had he used a musket and pistols? Or was he one of the thieves William talked about, looking to ransom the wife of the governor of Normandy? Perhaps he was saving her for his own ends.

By the time the first rays of sunlight made their way through my bedroom window, I was wide awake. I was already dressed and ready to go. I made my way down the spiral staircase to find Barkslow and half a dozen men gathering up equipment and carrying it outside. It looked like they were going on an expedition and didn't expect to be back soon.

"Good, you're awake. We need to get moving. Your team has been fed and rested," Barkslow said. "Would you prefer to ride one of our horses and leave your carriage here?"

"I'll take the carriage. Inside the coach will be the safest place for her," I said.

Barkslow nodded, and we all went outside. Lord Parlimae was already there, standing at the bottom of the steps. There was one wagon with a two-horse team, plus six horses saddled and ready to go.

The men filled up the wagon with their supplies: steel traps, extra firearms, ammunition, netting, water, and food. They mounted their horses and waited for the order to depart. Barkslow monitored the progress, then turned to me. "I didn't think you would leave the carriage. I placed an extra musket next to your seat. I cleaned and loaded it as well."

My cheeks heated. The number of things we'd kept from them was getting a little embarrassing.

"We will split up. I will lead four of the men to the sea to retrace the rider's horse. Hopefully, we can pick up the trail. Shouldn't be too hard at first, soft sand and all. We'll take our wagon in case we need to transport her in it." Barkslow looked at me as he continued. "Three men will go with you to Mercel. Learn what you can. Maybe he took her there. If he is a highwayman, he may send a ransom from there. Don't dawdle in Mercel. Learn what you can, be quick about it, and return back to the castle. It is truly the only safe place in the entire valley. We will meet here by sundown. Don't get caught out there after dark."

"There's no point in coming back here," I barked.

Lord Parlimae's voice was quiet, but it grabbed my attention. "Listen, child, if they detect tracks, they will follow it until they either find her or lose the trail. That will take all day. It will take you half a day to get to Mercel, and it will not take you long to determine if she is there or if anyone knows this rider. Either way, both teams need to return here with her or with new leads. You need to work together to find her."

I nodded my head slowly. They were right again. I just didn't like all the waiting and wasted time. Who knew how far away he might have taken her by now. Part of me wanted him to have taken her out of this dangerous land. The other part wanted to find her quickly and return.

I snapped the reins and directed Arca across the drawbridge and through the valley toward the forest. Three riders on horseback followed behind. I kept the pace nice and steady. As much as I wanted to hurry to Mercel, I couldn't overstress the horses.

We stopped at the crossroads, and Barkslow drew up next to me. "Don't worry," he said with a smile. "We'll find her. These men are at your disposal. You'll be safe with them. Don't be afraid to use the muskets if you need to. If one of us isn't back by nightfall, we've either found her or are on our way to finding her. Good luck."

With that, Barkslow spurred his horse. He and his men took the road to the east, which led to the sea. I snapped the reins and turned my team toward Mercel. Before long, we crossed the entrance to the forest. The three riders kept pace easily but stayed well behind the coach.

We rode for a couple of hours before we came to a small creek, which mi Lady and I had passed as we fled Mercel. The horses needed a breather and a quick drink, so I stopped. I pulled the horses up to the creek, and the three men gave their horses a drink too.

One of the horses carried a large net, which seemed to glimmer with silver thread. Restraints dangled off another horse. They too shone like silver.

My companions seemed on edge. One of them, a tall, thin man, narrowed his eyes at me. "What happened last night?"

I knew they heard most of my story when I arrived at the castle. I wasn't sure why he was asking. Maybe it was just small talk, or maybe he missed some of the conversation. "You mean the murders in Mercel?" I asked.

He shook his head. "No, I mean in the forest. Just exactly what did you see?"

He had heard my entire account when I told Lord Parlimae and Barkslow. This question was about something else. It was as if he knew I was holding back. But how could he? We'd been alone when the werewolf saved us.

"I told you everything last night," I said.

He turned his head to one of the other men. They exchanged a glance that suggested they knew better. The men mounted their horses, waiting impatiently for a few moments before trotting off.

I didn't care if they knew I was holding back. I certainly wasn't the only one keeping information to myself. I climbed into the driver's seat, snapped the reins, and guided the team across the creek. I pulled up to the rider who had been speaking to me.

"What is it you're not telling *me*? Why do you have nets and restraints?" I asked.

The rider looked over at me and then back at his buddies. With great reluctance he said, "William, Lord Parlimae's son, did not come back last night. He went for a late ride and did not return. If the stranger had anything to do with it, we will need to capture him."

The other two riders avoided my gaze. They tried to act as if they didn't hear our conversation, but I knew better. The men weren't supposed to tell me about William.

I nodded in understanding, then snapped the reins to push the team faster. We picked up the pace, the carriage leading the riders through the gloomy forest.

My mind wrestled with the news about William. Was he somehow involved in all this? Could he be the werewolf? If so, why would he have questioned mi Lady's story? He hadn't acted as if he shared her secret; he seemed to know something she didn't.

It was equally strange that both he and mi Lady were missing. I knew William wasn't the blond-haired stranger that saved her from the pack, but where was he?

There was no trouble on the way to Mercel. The pace was fast, but it was peaceful. The only odd thing I noticed was how eerily quiet the forest was. Not a single bird chirped.

When we pulled into town, there wasn't a soul around. The streets were bare. The livery appeared closed. The town resembled the village outside Castle Parlimae when the peasants had sheltered within the castle walls.

I pulled the team up to the inn and set the brake. The riders hitched their horses in front of the building and dismounted. Each grabbed his musket. I led two of the riders into the inn. The third stayed just outside the door. He would watch the street and alert us if anything happened.

The place was empty like the night we first came, but it lacked the murmur of voices from the tavern below. I walked over to the counter and rang the bell. I listened intently for any movements or sounds. The inn was silent. I rang the bell again, but the innkeeper never appeared.

I looked at the two men and then walked behind the counter to the staircase that led to the pub. We found some pints on the bar, a few glasses on tables, and half-eaten dinners. But no townsfolk. They hadn't even bothered to clean up from the night before.

I motioned for the two men to follow me. We exited through the door that led to the alley. The man guarding the horses joined us.

"I haven't seen a soul out here. Something is really wrong," he said.

"The inn and pub are empty too," I added.

In the silence that followed, the men looked around the alley with wide, unbelieving eyes. The bodies were gone, probably cleaned up by the townsfolk. But the destruction remained. The swath of blood still stained the wall, and bits of flesh and fur clung to the hold in the fence. The large claw marks behind the splatter of blood seemed to disturb them the most.

There weren't that many houses in this small village, but it was strange not to see any activity. We should have seen someone on the street or at home.

As we walked up the main street, we passed the only store in Mercel. The front door was ajar, something I hadn't noticed when we passed earlier. I stepped inside and called out, but nobody answered.

"Something else must have happened," I said as I strode onto the street. "Who would leave all these goods unattended?"

"We should go," said one of the men.

I shook my head. "We have to find her. She could be here hiding."

We kept walking toward the livery at the end of town. A murmur of voices came from the barn, soon accompanied by the sound of people moving about. Two of the men fanned out to watch either side of the barn, the hammers on their muskets cocked and ready to fire. The tall man stayed at my side.

I tried to pull the large entrance doors aside, but they wouldn't budge. At once, all noise from within stopped.

"Who's there?" said a voice from inside the barn.

Someone else whispered, "Quiet, Sam. Are you crazy?"

"It's OK. We're here to help," I yelled through the doors.

The barn door jiggled. A few clangs later, it opened a crack. A short, chubby man peered out. He looked us over and, with a sigh of relief, opened the door.

It looked like the whole town was inside—about twenty people, I guessed. There were a few women huddled next to their children and some horses tied in stalls. The chubby man stepped into the open and looked around cautiously.

"Is it only you two?" he asked hesitantly.

"And our two companions, who are around the barn. They're from Castle Parlimae. How long have you been in there?" I asked.

A few more of the men stepped outside, and the women all stood, taking a few steps toward the door. The chubby man still had a look of concern on his face as he spoke. "We've been in here most of the night."

"What happened?" I asked.

"There were two murders," said the chubby man—Sam, I presumed. "The Tandeauxs were killed in the alley beside the inn. They were in the pub, had a fight, and went outside only to be torn apart by some monster—wolves, maybe."

"That was them in the pub?" I asked. The bodies had been so badly mutilated I hadn't recognized them as the couple that fought in the pub that night.

At Sam's questioning look, I clarified. "I was here. Mi Lady and I left right after. We were afraid to stay." I searched the crowd of men, a furrow forming between my brows. "Where's the innkeeper? What happened to him?"

"We ain't seen him. Not since the other night," Sam said. "You were the wise ones. Most of the men from town decided to follow the Hessians as they went after the killer. None of them returned. Maybe the innkeeper went with them.

"Sometime in the early morning hours, just before the dawn, something surrounded our village. Howls pierced the night. We thought they were wolves, but no wolf makes a sound like that." He swallowed hard. "A couple of townsfolk left the bar to investigate. We found their corpses behind the doc's place. Torn to shreds, just like the Tandeauxs."

He lowered his head as tears began fall. His voice trembled at the memory. "We all gathered and started to account for one another. The owner of the general store and his clerk were mutilated. We found them in the stockroom of the store. The owner's head was severed from his body. The boy, Jean Paul, he was gutted and staked to a wall."

I remembered the grocer and his clerk from the bar that night. They'd been eating supper together. Both had seemed quiet and innocent.

Sam pulled himself together. "We all decided to come here. It's the safest place in town. There are no windows, and the two doors are the only exits. We barricaded the doors just in time. Something kept trying to get in. The doors shook violently for hours, first the front, then the back. On and on. We didn't think the doors were going to hold, especially after seeing what the monster did to the fence in the alley.

"Each time it failed to get in, it let out a loud, bloodcurdling scream. None of us thought we were going to make it. Right before sunup, the doors stopped shaking and the noises quit. We were too afraid to come out. We decided to stay in here awhile longer, or until the Hessians and the rest of our men returned." He looked at me, confused and scared. "Why did you come back?"

"I'm looking for the lady I was with. Did you see her? Is she here somewhere?" I questioned.

Sam shook his head. "I'm not sure who you mean, but there are no strangers in here. Only townsfolk. What happened to her?" he asked.

"There was a stranger in the pub that night. Tall, blond-haired man with a trimmed beard. Do you know him?" I asked.

"No," he said. "What does that have to do with her?"

"I think she may be with him," I stated.

Sam shared a loaded look with the group of townspeople. His eyes flicked to mine. "That's the same man who killed the Tandeauxs."

My gaze fell, and so did my heart—but not because I worried the blond man was the killer. Though one witness described him standing over the bodies, another had spotted the black wolf in that alley. And my money was on the black wolf.

Right now, I was more concerned that she wasn't in Mercel. And that the townsfolk had no useful information to share. We had to go back, but we couldn't leave these people unprotected. They had no weapons except for a few pitchforks and hatchets.

I looked at the tall man from Castle Parlimae. "Somebody needs to stay here and protect these people."

He nodded his agreement. "Two of the men can stay behind. I'll ride with you back to the castle. We'll get reinforcements and come back."

"You should stay too. If I can make it back to the castle by nightfall, I should be fine. They're going to need all the help they can get. Besides, I travel faster by myself," I said.

He hesitated, then reluctantly agreed. He walked me back down the street to the carriage. A few of the townsfolk hurried to the store with the other guards. As I climbed into the driver's seat, I saw them carrying supplies back to the livery.

The tall man spoke just before I left. "Be careful and don't delay. You have to get back to the castle by night, or it won't be safe."

Nodding, I kicked the brake free. I turned the team around and snapped the reins for Arca to move a little faster. As he did, I yelled back to the tall man, "Keep them safe. I'll meet Barkslow and send help."

I snapped the reins even harder to put Arca and the rest of the horses in full gallop. We plunged into the darkened forest, heading east once again.

# EIGHT

# THE
# ABANDONED CHURCH

*A*rca and the team bolted down the road. A plume of dust trailed the carriage. It would prevent me from detecting a rear attack, but I was more concerned with speed.

My mind was racing almost as fast as the horses. I needed to get back to the castle and send help to the people of Mercel. I was so focused on my task that I almost missed it: an odd break in the trees up ahead.

As we got closer, I realized it was an old road that branched to the left of the main thoroughfare. I hadn't noticed it on the way here. I pulled the reins back and stalled the team right at the opening.

Although ferns covered the ground, I made out a distinct trail. Some of the vegetation was crushed, like something had trampled it recently. I stared down the path of flattened undergrowth to where it disappeared between the row of trees.

Someone had traveled here. I doubted it was Barkslow. He had several men with him. Their horses would have trampled most of these ferns. And they had a wagon with wheels that would leave a recognizable impression.

The Hessians and the townsfolks had even bigger numbers. They would have created a swath going through here. That would be hard to miss.

This was a single animal. And a large one—big enough to cause this trail.

Maybe it was mi Lady and the stranger. Were they at the end of this trail? The day was getting on, and this detour would hold up my return to the castle. I couldn't afford to delay sending help back to Mercel. The townsfolk only had three muskets.

Despite all that, I had to investigate. It didn't look like anybody else had picked up on the trail. If that were the case, and if mi Lady had traveled this path, I would be her only hope right now. The three guardsmen would just have to hold out with the townsfolk. Three muskets would have to do.

The path was too narrow for my big carriage. I didn't know what was up ahead, but if there were any sharp turns, we wouldn't make it through. The coach was also heavy. Any soft ground, and we could get stuck. As much as I didn't want to, I had to unhook Arca.

He was the best horse on the team—the strongest and most loyal. I didn't have a saddle, so I'd have to ride bareback.

I left the rest of the horses with the carriage. They would be fine, provided I wasn't gone for too long. I left the brake off so they could escape if attacked.

I hopped on Arca and pulled the reins, directing him down the trail. I slung the extra musket over my shoulder while keeping mine at the ready. I didn't want to be on this trail all day, so I spurred him to move at a nice trot.

The trail was fairly straight. It was a little easier to follow as I got further away from the carriage. Somebody had tried to cover their tracks where the trail met the road but was less thorough as the path traveled deeper into the forest. The ferns and forest undergrowth were even more pressed down here.

Arca and I went a couple of miles, stopping when we came to a small hill. The path rose over the mound. It was high enough that I couldn't see the other side.

Before reaching the top, I dismounted. With Arca in tow, I followed the trail. I thought it might be best to scout the area before riding ahead.

When I crested the hill, I scanned the land before me. Dense, dark forest prevented me from seeing too far, but I could make out the flat ground at the bottom of the hill and a small inlet. There, partially hidden within a thick pine grove, was a small church. It looked run-down and abandoned.

The trail led right to the church and circled to the back. I climbed up on Arca and guided him down the hill, walking him to keep the noise down. There was an opening in the trees on either side of the path. It looked like there might have been an old village here.

I moved the musket from my back to my side and carried the other musket in my hand. If I encountered trouble, I could get off two shots quickly.

We reached the church a few moments later, and I pulled Arca to a stop. I dismounted slowly and tied his rein to a nearby tree. I didn't want him taking off if he got startled.

It was quiet, just a few birds chirping in the trees. My heart pounded with fear. Still, this wasn't as nerve-racking as what I experienced when the wolves were nearby.

The church was small and made of gray stone. Moss climbed its sides. It had a high steeple and tall stained-glass windows. The tall front doors were closed, and there was debris on the front steps. The building looked empty, but someone—or something—might be waiting inside to ambush me.

Using the front door seemed too obvious, so I walked around the side, following the trail. It stopped just before a door at the rear of the building. It was slightly ajar, revealing a dark interior.

My heart was pounding even louder now. I pushed the door with the barrel of my musket. It swung inward with a groan. I peered around what appeared to be a small room at the back of the church. It looked empty, so I took a cautious step. The floor gave a bit, and the wood let out a squeak. It was the kind of creak that alerted everyone to an intruder.

I rolled my eyes and shook my head in disbelief. I was trying to be quiet, and so far, I had managed to make two loud noises upon entering: the door and the floor.

The room was in some disarray. A bed lay at the far end, next to a fireplace with ashes in the hearth. A few chairs and some dinnerware were strewn throughout the room. Some busted-up pieces of wood and glassware lay scattered on the floor.

I moved to my right and peeked through another door. It led to the sanctuary, and I stepped in. I was alone, and I relaxed some. My heart rate returned to normal, which alleviated the pounding in my ears.

I was standing in the back of the church. The numerous pews were dusty but otherwise undisturbed. They led to an altar at the front of the sanctuary.

As I turned to go back outside, I heard a faint voice. It scared me half to death, and I instantly raised my musket. My eyes became focused.

"Seth? Is that you?" a woman whispered.

The sound was coming from the sanctuary, but where? I waited a few seconds without moving. Maybe I had imagined it.

The whisper came again. "Seth? Is that you?"

Now I was sure I'd heard it. And this time, I recognized the voice. "Mademoiselle?" I called out.

A loud creak emanated from the floor beside me. The sound was so abrupt I nearly jumped out of my skin. A door in the floor lifted. It was her, revealing mi Lady.

I set the musket down and quickly grabbed the door, pulling it off of her. She climbed up the ladder into the room. Instinctively, I reached out and hugged her. Tears streamed down my cheek, but I regained my composure and stepped back.

"Forgive me, mademoiselle," I said, wiping the tears from my eyes.

She sighed in relief and put a hand on my shoulder. "It's so good to see you," she said as she hugged me.

She pulled back and walked to the church's front doors, cautiously looking outside. She scanned the forest as if trying to find someone—probably the "Seth" she'd called out to. Was he the blond-haired rider?

I picked up the musket and walked outside. "We must get going, mi Lady. There isn't much time, and we need to get back to the carriage as quickly as we can if we are to make Castle Parlimae by nightfall."

Together we rushed to Arca. I mounted first, then pulled her up. "Come, Arca. Show us how fast you really are."

Arca carried us up over the hill as swift as ever. Within no time, we were back at the carriage. Mi Lady hopped off the horse and climbed inside the carriage while I harnessed Arca. As I went to get back into the driver's seat, mi Lady slid the carriage window open and said, "We're not going to Castle Parlimae."

I looked at her with wide eyes. "We won't make it anywhere else before nightfall, mademoiselle."

"We need to go back to the beach," she ordered.

"Why?" I asked.

"Trust me." It was all she would say.

Reluctantly, I climbed into my seat and directed the team forward. Mi Lady was in a hurry, but it hadn't turned out so well the last time we were at the beach. I did trust her, though. Still, it would be best if we arrived before nightfall.

It wasn't long before we came to the edge of the forest and the foothills of Castle Parlimae. Instead of following the road north to the castle, I turned east at the crossroads as she had asked. This would take us back to the sea.

The road was smoother in the valley, allowing us to go a little faster. And the tiny breeze behind us gave an added push.

The sun was beginning to set behind us. I couldn't see the village that clearly from here, but I turned to look at the castle anyway. The soft light of evening made it look quiet.

The peacefulness didn't last for long. The forest ahead looked darker, and it came up quickly. When we reached the trees line, we crossed over from light to dark. The sun had disappeared behind us, and the moon was making its rise. Moonlight squeezed through the foliage, offering scant illumination for our ride.

This was as long a section of the forest as the one at the beginning of our journey. It would be a while until we made our way through. The team had been running a long time and needed a break. I'd really pushed them through the valley so we could cross without any-body noticing.

I slowed the horses from a gallop to a trot, and kept the pace steady. The road was smooth, which made it easier on the carriage. The thick trees blocked the wind, so we didn't meet any resistance.

After traveling for a couple of hours, we were about halfway to the sea. A freshwater creek ran across the road, and I stopped the carriage. The horses were tired from the hurried pace and needed a drink.

Hopping down, I hustled to the front and made sure Arca and Killian were in position to drink. When they were finished, I pulled them ahead so the second set of horses could drink.

Mi Lady got out of the coach and looked around cautiously.

"I just need to give them a breather, mi Lady," I said.

"It's OK. He will find us," she replied.

"Who will find us?" I asked. "What happened, mi Lady, if you don't mind my asking? I searched all over for you."

Mi Lady looked around the dark forest. She stared at the moon through the treetops. With some reluctance, she met my eyes. "His name is Seth," she said. "I knew him as a child. William, Seth, and I grew up together in this valley. We used to play together as children. But I had not seen them since I left this land many years ago."

She took a deep breath, steeling herself. "When the wolves attacked us at the beach, it was Seth who saved us. He was the masked rider. When his bullets did not kill the black wolf, he knew he had to get me out of there fast. That was when he decided to pick me up, get on his horse, and ride out.

"The buckskin horse ran all the way to the church where you found me. Seth carried me into the back and laid me on a bed there. My head injury and other cuts put me into a fever. He covered me with blankets, gathered wood, and started a fire to keep us warm.

"Once we were safe in the church, he spent more time cleaning the wounds on my leg and arm. Seth had learned the art of healing. He boiled some water and stitched me up with some of his horse's hair. He used some type of herbal ointment on my wounds to speed up the healing, along with something else I did not know about at the time.

"Between the pain and the fever, I passed out. I'm not sure how long I was asleep, but when I awoke, it was still dark. As my eyes adjusted to the dim light from the fire, I noticed the door to the sanctuary was open. I could see Seth sitting in one of the pews, staring at the large cross behind the altar. He saw that I had awakened and walked back to the room.

"'You should save your strength,' he told me. I lay back down and looked up at him. He sat on the side of the bed and wiped my brow with some cool water.

"It was hard for me to speak, but I managed to ask, 'Where am I?'

"He told me I was safe. That they did not know where I was now.

"'Who?' I asked.

He said it was the pack,

"I started to remember. Images of the attack at the beach worked their way into my memory. If it weren't for him, I would be dead. I looked up at him, and he smiled. He squeezed a bloody cloth into a nearby basin. Dipping the rag in clean water, he wiped my face again. I watched him intently as he took care of me.

"The fire put a soft glow over the entire room. I drifted back to sleep. When I awoke, Seth was standing at the window, staring at the moon.

"'You saved me, just like you did all those years ago,' I said to him.

"He looked over at me with soft eyes. He said nothing. A small smile came across his face as he turned to look back at the moon.

"'It is you, isn't it? I thought you had died all those years ago,' I said.

"He looked back at me. His eyes dropped to the floor, as if he was remembering. He looked back and nodded slightly.

"He spoke as he walked back to me and told me that I should not have come through this country. He pulled up a seat next to the bed and sat down.

"'My grandmother is ill. I was on my way to Trevordeaux. You remember her, don't you?' I asked him.

"He nodded that he did before he spoke again, telling me it would have been better if I had taken the road to the north and not come through the forest.

"'Is my driver dead?' I asked.

"He said you were fine, and called you very brave. He said most others would have run off but that you stayed and tried to protect me. He said this proves nobility is not about your title.

"'You have been alive all this time. Why didn't you come back to me? Why did you stay away? What happened to you? I have so many questions,' I said.

"Seth turned away and looked back at the fire. There was great pain in his eyes. It looked as if memories flooded into his mind—painful memories. He moved closer and took my hand. My eyes filled with tears and my heart began to beat faster. It was hard to breathe.

"What he told me next was something he had not told anyone before. Only a few people knew what happened to him. He never wanted to burden anyone with this story.

"He took a deep breath before he spoke. He reminded me of an incident long ago when I was riding alone in the fields. It was the day the black wolf attacked me.

"As he was speaking, I began to remember things I had not thought about in a long time. It was a beautiful day. The autumn's chill was in the air, but it was still warm. The sun was out, and the birds were singing. I was supposed to help my grandmother with some chores. The harvest was right around the corner. She told me to take the old mare out for a ride, that it would do the horse some good.

"I saw Seth working in the fields. I rode up to the castle to find William, but he wasn't around. After that, I rode out through the valley to see how long Seth was going to be.

"I was passing a small mound of tall grass when a black wolf jumped me. The force knocked me off my horse and the old mare galloped away in a panic. The wolf's claws raked across my shoulder and up my neck, drawing spurts of blood. My collarbone broke beneath its weight.

"I struggled to sit up, screaming for help. The wolf knocked me to the ground. This time, he pinned my arms down with his giant paws. I squirmed and tried to get free, but he was too strong. I thought he was going to kill me.

"Out of nowhere, Seth ran at the wolf and stabbed him with his pitchfork, knocking him off me. I watched as Seth fought him. He had used the pitchfork to keep his distance, but the wolf was too much for him.

"I watched in horror as he was mauled by the black wolf. I saw his body go limp. I thought he killed Seth as he dragged him through the weeds. That was the last time I saw him. I thought he was dead.

"Seth responded slowly, telling me that he felt dead in all the ways that matter. It was as if he had been killed by the black wolf.

"He said he had been tying straw bales together in the field when he heard my screams. I was yelling for help, so he ran to me as fast as he could. It looked like the black wolf was about to kill me when Seth charged. He thrust the pitchfork into the beast's side as hard as he could. The creature's hide was too thick for the prongs to penetrate deeply. He was too powerful to kill, but the force of Seth's blow did knock him off me.

"He tried to use the pitchfork to keep the wolf at bay, but the black wolf swatted it away as he turned to attack Seth. The force of his jaws clamping down on Seth's shoulder crushed bones. The attack was so fast and brutal Seth passed out.

"Seth said he remembered being dragged off through the weeds. He kept falling in and out of consciousness as he was pulled into the forest. He had lost so much blood that he prayed for a quick death because as he didn't have any strength to fight. Then the black wolf suddenly let go.

"He had been shot. A father and son had been hunting red deer in the woods when they saw the wolf dragging him into the woods. The young boy fired first. As his musket ball hit the black wolf, his father fired a second shot, narrowly missing. They reloaded, preparing to fire again, but the black wolf ran off.

"As he was telling me this, I began to remember more of the black wolf's attack. I'd been scared to die, so scared I heaved myself off the ground and tracked down the mare. I climbed astride and raced to the castle. People rushed at me from everywhere, shocked by the sight of my injuries. The doctor bandaged my wounds as I told them what had happened.

"When Lord Parlimae heard my story, he ordered the doctor to take me into the castle. Then he left with some of his men to look for Seth. Hours later, they returned. They had found only blood, no sign of Seth.

"I stared at Seth in disbelief and told him, 'We had all given up hope. How are you here now? How did you survive?'

"Seth walked back to the window. He looked up at the moon. What he told me next was something so strange I could hardly believe it," mi Lady said. Her expression was grave. "After everything that has happened, I know it has to be true."

# NINE

# THE TRAVELLERS

The story mi Lady was telling me would be hard for anyone to believe. But she was right: after everything that had happened to us on this trip, I knew anything was possible.

As she kept talking, some things were starting to make sense. From the moment I pulled the carriage into Castle Parlimae, I knew she had a history there. Secrets.

I had learned of her connection to both Lord Parlimae and William, but I hadn't realized how well she knew them. I had suspected that the werewolf, wolf, and masked rider fit into her past in some way, and I was finally learning the connection through her story about Seth.

The next part of her story was no less remarkable. In fact, it was beyond anything I could have imagined. But I had no reason to doubt her.

She watched the moon as she continued with the tale. "Seth took a deep breath before he went on with his story. It was as if he was gathering his courage. Finally, after some hesitation, he said the hunters who saved him were members of a people you would call Travellers. Those who live in the Dark Forest prefer to be called Travellers.

"For hundreds of years, many have tried to exterminate them. For this reason, they don't like to draw attention to themselves or reveal the location of their camps. Travellers avoid detection by steering clear of civilization as much as they can. Their camps are always away from heavily used roads. The camp the hunters took him to was several miles farther in the forest.

"He said Travellers are from everywhere, yet from nowhere. They're forced from their homelands and made to wander without any place to call their own. They are a group of people from many lands with a distinctive culture and their own set of traditions. Most of their rules revolve around doing things that are honorable.

"They're not beholden to any one government or crown. They survive by living off the land. The women forage, while the men hunt for all types of meat. Some earn money by providing services to outsiders, such as singing or dancing. Seers of the group read fortunes by use of a special deck of cards. Others are salesmen or craftsmen, each earning income that goes toward items needed by the community—things they cannot forage for themselves.

"Each Traveller community has its own king, who is elected for life. This is someone who they respect and obey. He protects them and guides them. He does everything our nobles are supposed to do, but unlike them, he doesn't let greed and arrogance fog the memory of his duty. Traveller kings are beholden to their people, but their rules are law. And one of those laws forbids Travellers from bringing strangers into the community. This places them all at risk.

"But the young hunter urged his father to break the rules. Seth was badly wounded and barely alive. The boy respected all life and was moved to protect Seth. This boy would later become Seth's brother.

"The father carried Seth straight to the *drabarni*, the medicine woman of the community. She had one of the larger wagons in the caravan. It was big and red, with gold trim and ornate carvings all over the structure. A small porch on the back led to a door with frosted windows.

"The healer was a woman of great importance and respect among the people. She took Seth inside and tended to him for days. The first thing she did was stop the bleeding. Using thin pieces of twine, she made ties around the cuts on his limbs. Once the bleeding slowed, she used pure water and cloth to wash out the lacerations.

"When the bleeding had stopped and the wounds were clean, she stitched the openings back together. The pain from her sewing was so severe he passed out. As she continued to work, the pain revived him. Seth couldn't remember how long he went on like that, awakening and fainting again and again.

"After his wounds were stitched, she formed a paste with some herbs and mosses she gathered from the forest. She combined that with some mud-like clay before coating his injuries and wrapping them in more cloth.

"Seth developed a fever, along with cold sweats. The *drabarni* placed cold rags over his forehead to cool his body. He was at the edge of death. She kept vigil at his bedside day and night. He remembered the smell of burning sage, the sound of her prayers, and the feel of fresh, clean bandages against his skin.

"After a few days, the fever broke. The bleeding had stopped, and his wounds began to heal. He improved a little each day. Some of the Travellers believed her magic had healed him. Others thought he was touched by black magic. The skeptics wanted him gone, but she wouldn't let them cast Seth out or harm him.

"The Travellers knew he'd been marked by the beast. The black wolf isn't an ordinary wolf. He is the spawn of evil, a hideous creature whose sole purpose is to kill. The Travellers tell a legend of such creatures, the first of which emerged after a man was cursed by a witch. The beast was her revenge gone wrong. Her action has devastated thousands for centuries.

"Some of the Travellers come from the Romani, a nomadic people who reside in a region to the east, beyond our borders. They speak of a place called Wallachia. This has a mountainous landscape surrounded by dense forests just like this one.

"The king of Wallachia was a cruel man. Invaders, assisted by some of his subjects, attacked his castle. The invaders were defeated and vanquished, but they killed his family during the conflict. The loss of his family drove him mad. He sought revenge.

"The king knew of an English custom called jus primae noctis. This allowed nobles to sleep with their peasants' brides on their wedding night. He resented his subjects and decided to inflict the most heinous punishment he could imagine: he made jus primae noctis law.

"Some saw this as an opportunity to fill the land with more noble blood. Others were just wicked and cruel men whose lust overtook reason. Many of the lords took full advantage of this despicable practice—including a nobleman in the southern region of Wallachia.

"He took many a young bride on her wedding night. Most of the peasantry in this small village submitted. But one young woman resisted. On the day of her wedding, he raped her. And her new husband was made to watch. Fearing the king's wrath, her neighbors and clergy from the church refused to come to her aid.

"Her husband could not bear the pain of what the nobleman had done. He anguished over the thought that he'd been unable to protect the woman he loved, and he hung himself in the pantry. This poor woman was devastated not only by the nobleman's assault but also by the loss of the love of her life.

"What nobody in the village knew was that she belonged to a secret coven of witches. Because witches are feared and scorned, they went to great lengths to hide. The penalty for practicing witchcraft is death, usually by drowning or burning at the stake. This woman had been recruited at a young age and practiced for many years.

"After she fell in love with the local blacksmith, she vowed to give up the practice of witchcraft. Jus primae noctis and the suicide of her husband changed all that. And soon it would change the world forever.

"She knew spells and incantations from the far reaches of the land. Her coven practiced both black magic and white. As the legend goes, she gathered her coven to cast a curse on the nobleman. Because he could not resist his primal, animal instincts, she would change him forever. Just as he did to her.

"Most societies fear wolves. They devastate livestock and threaten human existence. Their howls at night are terrifying to those who hear them. People will go to great lengths to hunt and kill entire packs when they are discovered.

"The witch planned to kill the nobleman. But first, she wanted him to feel her terror. She wanted him to know the devastating pain he caused her. He needed to experience what it was like to be hunted and chased. Then she would kill him.

"But she also resented her neighbors and the church. They needed to experience this fear as well. After all, they just stood by and did nothing.

"The coven collected the nobleman's blood. The witch mixed his blood with blood from her husband as well as blood from some other animals. Over a large black cauldron, the coven chanted and cast spells for days.

"When the moon had finally reached its highest point in the sky, they kidnapped the nobleman and brought him to their lair. They bound him, gagged him, and stripped him of his clothing. Holding the jawbone of a dead wolf, they dipped the teeth into the mixture of blood, which had been simmering in the cauldron. They raked the nobleman's body with the jawbone. The spell they cast on the mixture of blood caused him to pass out.

"When he awoke the next day, he was in bed within his castle. Believing the witches' ritual was nothing more than a nightmare, he didn't give it any more thought. But during the next full moon, everyone in the village learned how effective a witch's curse can be. As the moon arced to its zenith, the villagers heard an awful howl from the nobleman's castle. It was unlike the usual howl of wolves. This was deeper, painful, and terrifying—more monster than animal.

"That night, several villagers were killed. Their bodies were savagely torn apart. Later, villagers found half-eaten torsos with missing limbs, the arms and legs thrown in different directions. Some of the bodies were missing heads. Others had their eyes and tongues removed. The village was painted with the blood and guts of those who had done nothing to help the witch who was violated.

"Most of the villagers believed the dead had fallen prey to a pack of wolves. Since the deaths had been so gruesome, they thought the pack was probably diseased or rabid.

"As the months rolled by, the deaths continued. The villagers demanded answers from the nobleman. They wanted protection and found it odd that he would not help. Fearing for their existence, they formed hunting parties to kill any wolves in the area.

"The nobleman became afraid of being discovered, just as the witch had hoped. But something happened that the witch had not counted on. For you see, she was with child. Eventually, she gave birth to a baby boy.

"Before her husband took his own life, they had conceived a child. The nobleman believed the child to be his from his indulgence of jus primae noctis, a bastard child who might one day claim he was heir to the nobleman's lands. He also feared the child may be like him and would eventually try to kill him. This was not something he could tolerate.

"During the next full moon, the nobleman shifted into wolf form and burst into the witch's home. But she was ready for him, stabbing him repeatedly with a large knife. Each thrust hit a vital organ, yet the creature would not die. Her curse was the spawn of evil, a pact between the coven and the devil himself, and no ordinary weapon can kill evil.

"Her defense was in vain. With one blow, he flung her across the room, where she bounced off the wall. Injured and dazed, she could do nothing but watch the creature kill her child. He made a show of devouring the child so she'd see what her curse had done. He was more evil than she could have imagined.

"As a nobleman, he was already powerful. She had made him supernatural. And he embraced that power as the animal in him was unleashed.

"But the witch would not give up. The next day, she convened the coven. They waited until the nobleman left his castle. They spelled the guards, putting them to sleep, and entered.

"This nobleman valued power above all things. And to him, money meant power. His most precious possession was his collection of the purest of silver. While it was rare, he had accumulated a massive amount. The witches found a trove of it in his castle and took it back to their lair.

"After melting down the silver, they mixed it with more wolf blood. They cast a new curse on the smelted metal. They didn't just want to kill the creature; they wanted to kill him with the very thing he prized the most. So they forged weapons from the nobleman's silver: arrowheads, swords, spears, and knives.

"As the creature continued to kill across the land, the coven formed a hunting party. When the moon was full, the ocean tide high, and the stars bright, they hunted the beast. For three nights, they pursued him through the vast forest. They chased him until he finally returned to his castle. The witch waited inside. She shot three arrows into the creature. As the silver pierced his skin, he screamed in pain. But he did not die.

"The rest of the coven arrived just as he attacked the witch. They watched as he decapitated her. Enraged at the loss of their sister witch, they fired their arrows. This time, a silver arrowhead pierced the wolf's heart. The great beast fell where he stood, dying instantly.

"Once he was dead, his form returned to that of a man. That's when many of the villagers arrived. All they saw was their nobleman, naked, dead, and impaled by several arrows. The mob seized all but one of the remaining witches. They dragged them to the castle square, staked them to long poles, and burned them alive. Then they pursued the witch that escaped.

"The villagers followed her to the coven's lair. They found the cauldron, spell books, bones, and various herbs. The villagers destroyed all of it with fire.

"What none of them understood was that the nobleman had passed on his curse to others. Not all victims become infected, but those who do become creatures of the night. If the villagers had just read the books before they burned them or questioned one of the witches . . .

"This is part of why Seth could not return to the lands of Lord Parlimae. He also said it was why he could not return to me. He was changed forever, and the scars he bore would be known to anyone who saw them. They would know what he was, what he had become. This is what worried the Travellers.

"One night, the Travellers held a meeting. The king of the community had to decide if they were going to kill Seth, let him stay, or send him into exile. Seth was a stranger to them and a risk to their way of life. The king decided exile was not an option. They couldn't risk him telling others about them. They moved camp constantly, but they needed to remain a secret. More than that, they feared what he might do.

"He said the Travellers don't just tell stories. They believe their legends. None of them had seen him change, but they knew the tale too well. Convinced he was a night creature, they wouldn't let him roam the countryside to kill innocents.

"Most wanted to kill Seth. Those who favored that option wasted no time lobbying the king. It's not that they were bloodthirsty. They just thought his body was infected and his soul lost to the devil. To them, he was already dead.

"The father who found Seth pled for his life. He vowed to accept Seth as one of his own. If Seth became a danger to the community, he promised he would kill Seth himself. He was a good man and well respected by the community, so his words carried some weight.

"But it was the *drabarni* who really convinced everyone. Siding with the father, she told everyone she had consulted the cards. Although the legends are true, she said, there was something different about this case. Seth was not beholden to the evil one.

"She also spoke of another legend, a less-familiar prophecy that said a pale stranger would make the world safe for their people. She believed Seth was this stranger, which was why he had survived the attack. She explained that his lifeline was too strong.

"She reminded the community of the balance of all things. If the black wolf existed in all his evil, then a righteous wolf must exist to balance him. He was dark, and therefore, Seth was light.

"The king took a few days to think it over. On the third night, when the moon was waning, he told them of his decision. They would make Seth a part of their community. If the *drabarni* was wrong and the cards had failed, they would kill him. He ordered their blacksmith to prepare weapons of silver in case Seth became a threat.

"But they had another problem. The mystery of the wolf was well known among their people. There are other Traveller communities who know the legend. Outsiders were becoming familiar with it too. Anyone we encountered who saw Seth's scars would know what had happened and what he had become. They would surely kill him. But they might want to kill the entire community, fearing they were all werewolves.

"It was decided they would cover the scars with ink. Travellers enjoy covering their bodies with various adornments, such as jewelry and art. Most of it tells a story and has meaning. Other communities learn to recognize these ink markings when they encounter them. The symbols can also indicate who is friendly, who they are allied with, and who their enemies are. Each community has their own tattoo artist. Their styles can tell which community they belong to.

"When Seth was completely healed and his scars were well formed, the *drabarni* took him to the tattoo artist. For three days, Seth sat in his wagon as he covered the scars with ink. He wove the tattoo in a maze of black that masked the claw and bite marks on Seth's arms, chest and shoulders. But as Seth gained stature in the community, the artist added ink. Now the tattoos are a beautiful piece of artwork that tell a unique story.

"Hearing this, I reached up and opened Seth's shirt. I was amazed at the intricate details of the artwork. As I ran my fingers along the ribbons of black that engulfed his arms and chest, I could feel the scars. For the first time, I understood what I was seeing.

"When that tree fell in front of us as we fled Mercel, I knew it was him. I was right—he was the werewolf. The tattoos that marked his skin were identical to the black patterns that had covered the beast in the road and the wolf in the field.

"But Seth wasn't finished telling me all that had happened. He grew up in hiding. His new family kept him safe, but when the moon's light is full, the change consumes him. He was able to stay away during those times, keeping the community from seeing it.

"His life with the Travellers wasn't that different than it'd been in the valley. Seth and I were poor. We were peasants, while William was wealthy. Seth's Traveller family was the same. They had their own wagon, but it was small for a family of five. And they constantly worked to fill the pantry.

"Seth said for all the similarities, it was a different way to survive. Instead of doing everything for a lord, they took care of one another. The community survives by banding together. The men would hunt at various times of the day and night, providing enough meat for the entire group. They did repairs on the wagons and tended the horses.

"They had some livestock—mostly chickens and ducks. A few had goats to provide milk, meat, and something called cheese. Each day, somebody tended to the animals. Others gathered from the forest.

"The caravan moved a lot as they mostly stayed within the forest, taking the roads less traveled. Sometimes they would go into towns or cities to trade. Some of them would take jobs and learn different skills, bringing back new knowledge to the community. Seth learned how to heal, at least a little. He never achieved the status of a *drabarni*, but became skilled enough to help with my wounds.

"He said it was a good life. Each night after supper, they would visit different families and share stories around the campfire. Some would play instruments, others would sing, and most everyone danced.

"When he got older, things became more complicated. Another Traveller community invaded their area. Though they overtook several supply shipments, some of the king's men were able to defend their provisions. But the rival group's king was a clever man. He decided to wait until most of the men were away from camp.

"At that time, the camp was deep in the pine groves of the Dark Forest. They were near a large creek that ran swiftly over big rocks. Their wagons were lined up with their backs to the water.

"The rival group had watched from the other side of the river, patiently waiting for the men to leave. And then one night, they set out for a bullfrog hunt, which would've supplied meat for the entire community. That was when the rival group hit them. It was in the middle of the night, and nobody was prepared.

"Because the moon was full, Seth had already left the camp. He told me he can change form anytime he needs to, day or night. But when the moon is at its fullest, he cannot control the change. When the rival community attacked, Seth was mid-transformation. When this happens, his senses are sharp as a wolf. He knew something was wrong the moment he was completely changed. There was something in the air, a presence of evil.

"He made his way back to camp so he could see what was happening. When he got there, the attack was already underway. Several of the wagons were on fire. Their supplies had been raided, and men from the rival community were loading up their horses with their goods. His people had been hopelessly outnumbered and defenseless.

"Seth loved his new family and was enraged by the attack. He ran into the fight without giving it a thought. The opposing community was no match for what he had become.

"The lucky ones got out the moment they saw him, scared beyond reason. Those who weren't smart enough to flee were slaughtered. None of them had any idea of his connection to the camp.

"After he drove them off, he disappeared back into the darkness until morning. When he had changed back to a man, he returned to the camp. Though they had stayed in the camp, the king and his father had survived. But the few men who had remained to defend the camp were killed by the rival group.

"Most of the hunting party, including his brother, had returned by morning. Those who had been at camp shared everything about the attack—including the part about the wolf. They had recognized his tattoos and now knew how deadly he was. Even though he had defended them and drove off the attackers, they feared him.

"Word began to spread through the various Traveller communities. A mysterious beast had nearly killed an entire community during a conflict. Stories turned the battle into something bigger and grander than it actually was. That the beast had been defending one community from the assault of another was never spoken. All anyone heard was a story about a hideous beast killing men, women, and children.

"The community mourned their losses, rebuilt wagons lost to fires, and became stronger in the process. But in the end, they knew the problem was bigger than all of that.

"They could not risk associating with him. The king declared that it was necessary for Seth to leave the community. His father and brother failed to convince the king. Not even the *drabarni's* prophecy mattered. The community figured the prophecy had been fulfilled. A pale stranger had saved their community from the rival group.

"Ever since the day Seth was forced into exile, he crisscrossed the countryside looking for a home. There was just no place for him. He always worried his presence would cause others harm, so he stayed to himself. Mercel seemed as good a place as he would ever find. There aren't many people there. Road agents and highwaymen scour the land in search of victims, so anything unusual gets attributed to them.

"This is how he survived all these years. He kept to himself and blended in with the undesirables of the world. While he tried to forget the world and live in peace, Seth told me that he never forgot about us."

# TEN

# THE BLACK WOLF

Mi Lady's voice was filled with sadness as she told me all that had happened. She had loved Seth from the time they were young, growing up in the valley of Castle Parlimae. He was her first true love.

Seth had explained everything to her at the abandoned church. As she relayed his tale, I saw the heartbreak on her face. He had nearly died trying to save her. Despite the brutality of his own injuries, he managed to survive, only to be sentenced to a life of loneliness.

"I was trying not to cry as Seth was telling me everything, but it was overwhelming. Tears spilled over as he spoke," she said. And now as she was telling me, tears welled from her eyes. "Everything he was telling me was almost too much to bear."

She looked up at the moon again, seemingly lost in that moment with Seth. "I said to him, 'You have saved me three times from the black wolf. How did you know he would come after me again at the beach? After he attacked us on the road leaving Mercel?'

"Seth told me a few weeks before I set off on this journey, he was at the pub in Mercel. He was seated in the corner at one of the tables. A highwayman he knew came in and joined him. They had traded goods a few times and done some capers together.

"Seth had convinced the people of Mercel and some of the road agents he was a highwayman too. They didn't know anything about what he really was. He'd done a few jobs with some of them to survive.

"I was shocked. I looked at him and said, 'You rob people? That's why you had the mask on at the beach.'

"Seth gave me a serious look and said he never attacks the innocent. But he admitted to having looted shipments of goods going to Castle Parlimae. He wasn't proud of it, but everyone does what they have to in order to survive.

"I could see this bothered him. Seth looked down, as if he couldn't bear to meet my eyes. Then he told me a short time after that highwayman sat down, a few more of his companions joined them. One of them had just come from Normandy. He was scouting for jobs when he heard the story of a nobleman's wife who would be traveling soon.

"There was a rumor that this noblewoman was going to Trevordeaux, and in a hurry. Everyone knows the most direct route is through the center of the forest. The forest is so vast, and Mercel is the only place to resupply. Some of the road agents decided to wait near the inn to mark us when we arrived.

"As they sat there sipping ale, another highwayman said he had just come from the docks at Port Calibre to the east. He saw a new carriage being loaded onto a boat. It would travel over the seas instead of through the forest and mountains, arriving in Normandy within a few days. Not long after that, it would pick up a fare. Considering the opulence of the carriage, whoever rode in it would surely be worth a king's ransom.

"These highwaymen weren't the only ones to get information in Port Calibre. Seth had been there and ran into one of my grandmother's neighbors. Like many working families who used to live in the valley, she had moved to Trevordeaux and did business in Port Calibre. She told Seth of my grandmother's illness. He knew how close I was to her and that I would want to see her.

"Like the highwaymen, he suspected I would come this way. It is the most dangerous route to Trevordeaux, but it is also the quickest. When he heard of the fast and fancy carriage, he knew it had to be mine. After all, I am married to one of King Louis's favorite men in all of France.

"I grew up in the valley but have not been here in a number of years. It has gotten a lot more dangerous since then. So Seth decided to follow me from the mansion. That way, he could watch over me and make sure I was safe. That was how he was able to be there when the black wolf and his pack attacked us.

"As Seth was telling me all of this I immediately thought of the alley in Mercel. I looked up at him and asked, 'In Mercel, did you kill those people? A witness saw you in the alley over the bodies.'

"Seth took a deep breath, then said no. The black wolf had already attacked them. By the time he entered the alley, the black wolf had already killed them. When he saw Seth, the black wolf burst through the fence to escape. Seth chased him, but the black wolf disappeared into the mist.

"Seth had already told me that he did not return to the valley or me because of what he had become. But as I thought about it for a moment, I had to ask him, 'Why didn't you come back to me once you were healed? Our village wouldn't have cared about the scars. You know we don't believe in superstitions and curses. Your real family missed you.'

"Then, quietly, I added, 'And I missed you.'

"Seth looked at me with a raised eyebrow as he reminded me that I had seen what he becomes with my own eyes. Then he commented on my being a married woman now.

"I told him it was more complicated than that. Realizing Seth deserved my story after he'd laid bare his own, I said, 'My grandmother was heartbroken over what happened to me. She blamed herself for urging me to go riding that day. The scar on my neck was a constant reminder to her—to my whole family—of that fateful attack. They never thought I would find a husband.

"'And yet I did. Unfortunately, my husband requires someone who can provide him with heirs. That is something I can never do, so he is now looking for a new bride.'

"That's why I asked you not to call me duchess or your grace. Mi Lady is fine," she said to me. Mi Lady paused for a moment to look at the stars again before she continued.

"But Seth turned to me with a look of surprise. I think he realized that my life had not turned out as well as he had assumed.

"He knelt beside the fire, using the poker to stoke its embers a little. Then he added a few more logs to keep us warm. He rose and watched as it burned, the firelight reflecting off his face. He told me he couldn't have returned even if he had wanted to. By the time he was fully healed, Lord Parlimae had burned the village, forcing everybody out.

"When Seth said that my eyes went wide with disbelief. My mind raced to understand what he was saying. 'The fires that destroyed the village were accidents,' I said, though I heard the doubt in my voice. 'One of the chimneys caught fire, and it spread rooftop to rooftop, consuming each house until there was nothing left. We moved because my father found work in Trevordeaux.'

"Of course, as I repeated the story I'd been told, I thought about his version of events. More questions formed in my mind. 'Why would Lord Parlimae burn down his village?' I asked him. 'Those are the very people who supply his wealth. They tend the livestock, sow the fields with crops, and feed the entire land.'

"Seth sighed and said it was because Lord Parlimae knows the truth and can't bear to do the unthinkable, the one thing that he must do. No matter how many people have been butchered, he refuses to end the suffering.

"I am sure the look on my face mirrored the bewilderment I felt inside. I had no idea what Seth was talking about. I had never known Lord Parlimae to be cruel. That village had existed for generations under the Parlimae banner. What possible reason could he have had to burn it to the ground?

"Seth watched me, and I think he knew I was going to be shocked at the rest. But he had an incredulous look on his face, like he couldn't believe I didn't know any of this. Then he told me the biggest shock of all: the black wolf is William.

"My mind stopped. The words echoed in my brain. William was the black wolf? That didn't make any sense either. The three of us had grown up together. Seth was the oldest, William was next, and I was the youngest. The other children throughout the valley were much younger, making ours a natural friendship.

"Although William was the future lord of the land, he spent almost every day with us. Unlike Seth and me, he didn't have any chores or responsibilities, so he was free most of the time. We went fishing together and swimming on hot summer days. From time to time, William would take us hunting in the forest without his father's knowledge.

"And yet he attacked me all those years ago. I just couldn't make sense of it. Nor could I understand why he was still trying to kill me, so long after I left the valley.

"Seth could see I was frustrated and confused, so he told me the rest. I didn't like it, but I needed to hear it. All of it.

"He told me a story he'd learned long ago. Lord Parlimae didn't mind William spending time with us, but he always reminded William of his status and the obligations that came with his position. His dad would send some of the younger guards out with him on hunting trips. One day, they were hunting wild pigs deep in the forest. They rode horseback, using dogs to track and herd the animals into a good spot.

"They had been hunting these pigs for several weeks. They'd tracked the boars to the Great Eastern Forest, which lies several days from here.

"William shot one of the boars. The injured animal fled even further east, deeper into the forest. When William caught up to the boar, it was dead. He dismounted to admire his kill. Seth reminded me of how William always liked to boast of his prowess. We both knew that William enjoyed killing a little too much.

"He was right, of course. But that wasn't the end of Seth's tale. He said the thing nobody knew was that a pack of wolves had been tracking the wild pigs too. But this was no ordinary wolf pack. Their leader was a descendant of the curse. This pack had been following William and the hunting party from the moment they entered the wolves' territory. You see, wolves are good at hiding. You'll notice a wolf only when it wants you to.

"After William dismounted, a few of the men got off their horses as well. They were going to help him field dress the kill. That's when they were attacked.

"The hunting party had eight men, including William. Caught off guard, most of the men gave their lives to save William. He was attacked by the alpha but managed to kill it despite his injuries. It took nearly a week for the surviving men to get William back to the castle. They took the head of the great beast. They knew William would want the trophy if he survived. Seth pointed out this wolf's head was hanging in the dining room at Castle Parlimae.

"Nobody could have predicted what happened next. On nights when the moon was full, a great beast mutilated peasants in the village. For nearly a year, innocent lives were lost. And the villagers never knew William was behind the attacks.

"William seemed to target women more frequently. Many were found miles from their homes, half naked and torn to shreds. He chased them through the forest, enjoying the terror he elicited before he killed them. And, of course, he killed them in the most brutal way possible.

"It didn't take long for Lord Parlimae to figure it out. He wasn't a bad man, for the most part. He is uncharacteristically humble for a nobleman. He provided security and protection for the people of the village beyond what most do except in one regard. He couldn't bring himself to kill his only son, no matter how viciously William murdered his people. Instead, he brought on more guards. The peasants all thought it was to help them, but the truth was much different.

"That's why Barkslow is there. Parlimae hired him to captain the guards and contain William. To keep the beast from the valley, Barkslow forced him into one of the dungeon holds before the change. That didn't always work, and William sometimes escaped. When he did, the carnage was indescribable. His murderous rampages prompted some of the legends of this forest.

"With time, William got better at escaping. Barkslow wasn't able to contain him and finally hired the Hessians to kill William and destroy the pack. I was shocked at that revelation. I thought the king had dispatched Colonel Voelker to kill all the wolves. I told Seth how the Hessians had interrupted our breakfast at Castle Parlimae. How Voelker had a parchment with the king's orders with a wax seal from the king's signet ring.

"Seth just laughed. He said the king has no idea what is happening here. Barkslow finally had enough and hired the Hessians to exterminate all werewolves, including William. Unfortunately, this included Seth as well.

"Barkslow served with Colonel Voelker in the Americas during the colony uprising. He knew Voelker had encountered a creature there many years ago. And he knew Voelker wouldn't care who hired him as long as he got to kill night creatures.

"I told Seth that during our breakfast, neither Voelker nor Barkslow acted as if they knew each other. That was part of the ruse, Seth told me. He said Voelker and his men just arrived in Mercel two nights ago and asked if I remembered seeing them in the pub that night.

"I told him I did. Then I asked how he knew the Hessians had been hired by Barkslow and not the king. Seth said he'd heard Hessians were coming to the valley, so he went to the pub to see who they were meeting. That's when he saw me. He didn't want any of the road agents or highwaymen to see us together so he left abruptly. When I saw him in the pub it startled me. I wasn't sure it was him or if I was seeing things.

I believed he was dead. I thought it was just someone that looked like him. After he left, I ran outside to catch him, but he disappeared in the fog. So I went back to my room, convincing myself it wasn't him.

"It hadn't been a worthless endeavor on his part, though. He'd seen who the Hessians met with that night: a forger. Barkslow knows that Lord Parlimae would never allow them to hunt wolves on his land for fear they would discover the truth about William. But he also knows that Lord Parlimae is afraid of the king. A forged letter from the king would grant them access to his lands.

"Of course, Lord Parlimae didn't give up his son at the sight of the king's seal. He has successfully kept a lid on the truth for years. All he had to do was keep William under lock and key while Voelker and his men kill every doglike creature within a hundred miles. But as we now know, he relented in one way: he allowed them to hunt.

"After Seth told me about the pub, I was still a little confused. I didn't understand why William attacked me and Seth all those years ago—especially because we were all friends. But while it was a mystery to me, Seth knew the truth.

"William was obsessed with me, Seth said. He was consumed with the idea of making me his. Seth had seen William sneak into the forest to watch me take my morning rides. William had told Seth he fantasized about ruling the castle with me.

"I was so surprised. I asked Seth, 'Are you saying William was in love with me?'

"Seth told me it wasn't that simple. He didn't think William truly loved anyone but himself. He isn't sure William is capable of love. Seth believes William just wanted to possess me. William grew up with every advantage and could do whatever he wanted, but he couldn't have me, and that bothered him.

"Seth also told me Lord Parlimae knew of William's obsession with me. While Parlimae treated me like a daughter, I was not nobility. William needed to marry a girl with a proper bloodline to further their standing. He wasn't going to allow William to marry a peasant girl.

"William became angry and defiant. And then he learned how Seth felt about me. He knew we had grown closer, although he didn't know just how close we had become.

"He was determined to make me his girl. That's why he attacked. That is why he didn't kill me, Seth told me.

"I was puzzled by this. As I remembered it, the only reason I wasn't killed was because of Seth, and I told him as much.

"Seth told me that William could have killed me any time he wanted. He pinned my arms down to terrify me because fearful prey are the easiest to turn. Something about the fear helps them survive the brutality of their injuries. And they often turn.

"William wanted me to be his. He was going to turn me into a werewolf and member of his pack. That is why he didn't kill me. Seth interrupted him, and he had every intention of killing him for it. The Travellers unexpectedly saved Seth. His injuries were severe, and he stood on the precipice of death. Because of his fear—for me, for him-self—Seth became like William.

"William was infuriated that he didn't get to kill Seth. And when Lord Parlimae locked me away in the castle to heal, the frustration boiled over. William returned to the village and slaughtered Seth's real family. He tore apart his mother and father. Then he ripped the heads off Seth's younger brother and sisters.

"Lord Parlimae tried to cover that up. He ordered his most trusted guards to put the bodies back in the house and set it ablaze. But the guards didn't account for the heavy wind that night, and the fire spread. Within moments, the entire village had burned to the ground. The lord told everybody a chimney fire had spread out of control. In truth, the destruction was done to protect William.

"Then Seth told me my father was offered a job in Trevordeaux by an associate of Lord Parlimae. The lord wanted to get me and my family as far away from William as possible. William's obsession with me had already cost Lord Parlimae his village. Now he had to rebuild.

"William heard about my grandmother just as Seth did. He decided to wait near Mercel to see when I arrived. He planned to attack me before I could reach the village. But he was late getting there. We made it to the inn ahead of him.

"Some of his men were in the pub that night and saw me. They alerted William. He couldn't attack me in public, but he also couldn't wait too long. He wanted me to leave before sunup, so he killed those two people in the alley to get me to flee. William no longer wants to turn me into a werewolf. Now he just wants to kill me.

"William didn't know the Hessians were in Mercel or that Barkslow had hired them to kill him. Seth went into the alley to confront William but he fled. Voelker and his men were hot on their heels. Somehow Seth and William gave the Hessians the slip. Seth chased William miles away but William got away. Then he circled back to catch up with the carriage. That's when he knocked over the tree that blocked out path.

"I asked Seth why William ran if William wasn't afraid of him. But Seth said William isn't afraid of him. He said each time a werewolf kills, they absorb a little bit of the victim's energy. It makes them stronger, faster, and more powerful. William is far more powerful than Seth. Seth only kills those who deserve it, and he tries not to kill at all. William, on the other hand, is always hunting. In fact, he has gotten worse recently.

"It was so much information that I didn't know what to think. As much as I wanted to refute his version of events, I knew, deep down, that he was telling the truth.

"My memory of the first attack is not great. The injury I sustained left me half conscious, so my recollection of that day is hazy. I remember healing in the castle. I always believed I survived, at least in part, because of the kindness and compassion of the lord of the manor.

"But I had to admit it: Seth's account of the past was accurate. William was the wolf, and Lord Parlimae, while kind to me, had allowed his son to terrorize the land. I thought about that monster and asked, 'Why doesn't he look like you? Why is he always a black wolf?'

"Seth told me William prefers his wolf form because its more animal.

"I asked why William didn't die from the shots on the beach. I had watched a bullet graze his cheek and another lodge in his neck. He shouldn't have come back to life.

"Seth looked down again, somber and tired. He said werewolves can only be killed with silver through the heart. 'Any silver hurts their flesh, thanks to the witch's curse,' he said, his voice starting to fade. 'A silver chain can bind them, but it won't kill them. They suffer wounds from other weapons like everyone else, and it takes time for them to heal. But the only true way for a human to kill a werewolf is with a silver bullet to the heart.'

"'Why do you still have wounds from him if silver is the only thing that can kill you?' I asked.

"But Seth was too tired and told me to sleep. He whispered to me that was enough questions and I needed to sleep. He wanted me to rest and regain my strength. He told me we couldn't stay at the church for long and that the next day we would make our way to Trevordeaux. He promised to see me safely to my grandmother's.

"Then he placed his hand on my cheek. The touch was soft and warm. I leaned into his hand and closed my eyes. It was hard at first to find sleep. I was exhausted, too, but my mind would not shut down. Much of what I grew up believing was a lie.

"Just before I fell asleep, I looked over at him. He was standing at the fire. Watching him, I realized, I could never tell him."

# ELEVEN

# VILLAGE UNDER SIEGE

Mi Lady took a deep breath. She wiped a tear from her cheek. She had just told me a deeply personal and disturbing truth about who she was and where she came from.

But that wasn't the end of the story. She looked around the forest, her gaze finally landing on the stream running at our feet. Its burble was a soothing presence beneath the loud chirping of crickets. She sat on the step of the carriage as she continued with the rest of her story.

"The sound of hushed voices woke me up," she said. "I sat up, scanning the small room of the abandoned church. Seth stood just outside the door, talking to a young boy. The boy seemed emphatic and kept pointing toward the forest.

"After a few moments, the boy ran off, and Seth returned to the room. He studied me, as if making sure I was all right. The bleeding had long since stopped, and the wounds had healed nicely. I was feeling much better—stronger and more coherent. The things he'd told me and the events of this trip felt like a dream. In the light of the morning, I still struggled to understand how the story he told me the night before could be true. But I knew those things had happened, and it made me very sad.

"Seth put on his coat as he walked over to me. He placed a hand over my forehead and commented that my fever had broken. He checked my injuries and said that my wounds had almost completely healed.

"'How is that possible?' I asked.

"Seth told me that he used some of his blood in the ointment. He must have seen the look on my face because he immediately told me not to worry. He said it would not make me a werewolf like him. He said werewolf blood sometimes helps to heal others. It was one of the few good things to come from the curse.

"He sat back in the chair, his face turning to concern before he spoke. He said Mercel was under attack. The boy knew him and came to get his help. William had killed more of the people there. The pack trapped some of the townsfolk in the stables and were terrorizing them. He had to go back and help them.

"I didn't want to let him go. I flew into his arms as tears welled up in my eyes. I held on tight but knew he would not change his mind. He was going. He knew it was probably a trap, but he had to go.

"He was their best hope. He had to stop William. He wanted to end things in that alley a few nights ago, but the townspeople and the Hessians scared William off. He burst through the fence before Seth could get to him.

"Despite everything, Seth never wanted to hurt William. He looked down as he told me he was ashamed to say that for years he let William spill innocent blood, blaming his actions on the curse. Now, Seth could not sit by anymore. He had to get there before William kills the entire town. He wanted to end things once and for all, this night.

"'I thought you said he was more powerful?' I asked him.

"Seth looked at me and told me that he is, but that didn't make him invincible.

"Then he slowly pushed me back and stood up. He moved the chair and walked across the room, motioning for me to follow. Seth led me into the sanctuary, where he pulled open a hidden door in the floor.

"This trap door led to a secret compartment under the room. It was big enough for a couple of people to hide. There was a jug of water and a few candles. A small firebox sat in the corner, its pipe traveling underground and emerging away from the church.

"'Stay in here until I return,' Seth told me. He said if he was not back by midday, I was to take the road to the north. Go back to the sea where he drove off the pack. He said that if I saw anyone, to get off the road and hide. The pack has a keen sense of smell, but if they are in a hurry, they might miss me.

"At the sea, not far from where he found me, there is a cave in the big rocks. He said I could hide there until he arrived. He believed the opening was just big enough for me to squeeze through but didn't believe the pack could get in there. He told me to stay out of sight; he'd find me. Once this is over, he'd take me to Trevordeaux.

"Reaching out, I wrapped my arms around him again, tighter this time. I could feel the surge of emotion in him. I had wanted to hold him just one more time, but not like that.

"He pulled my arms from him and guided me down the ladder. When we reached the ground, he lit a candle to light up the room. Seth pulled a dagger from his belt and put it in my hand. 'If the wolf gets close enough for you to use this, you are probably already dead,' he told me. 'But if you can stab him in the heart, the blade will kill him.'

"Seth closed my fingers around the dagger. Surprisingly, the blade was black. 'I thought you said silver was the only thing that could kill him,' I said.

"'This is dark silver,' he told me. I had never heard of this before, so I asked him about it. He said, 'Any ordinary silver through the heart will kill a werewolf. Any silver that touches our skin will burn or cut us. But the metal used to make dark silver is special. It is hard to find and is very, very rare. It is the purest silver known to man.'

"'Where does it come from?' I asked.

"'The nobleman from Wallachia had the biggest stockpile of pure silver the world has ever known. Most believe the metal is found in the depths of the earth, far beyond where most men are willing to go. It's a place where the ground drives out impurities. What is left behind is the most beautiful ore there is,' Seth told me.

"Once it is smelted and folded, black magic is infused. The darkest of evils pour into the metal, turning the color from a shiny bright to the deepest black.

"The witches' magic was black, but they failed to pour all their evil into the silver. The silver they used to kill the nobleman didn't have enough evil in it. Since then, both good and bad men have sought a weapon to destroy night creatures.

"Nobody really knows who created dark silver. Some say it came from a wizard in Britannia who was trying to protect a gallant king. Others believe it was some Norsemen trying to impress a pagan god.

"The Travellers say life is about balance. Men like Seth, their affliction is not in balance with the known universe. They were spawned from an evil curse. Dark silver was created to restore that balance. Its evil goes way beyond the evil that exists in them, and this imbalance is something they cannot survive.

"It's why the blade turns black. Not even the beauty of silver can suppress the evil. A cut from one of these blades never heals. It never closes. You can stitch it together, but when the stitches are removed, the wound will open again. And cuts from a dark silver blade never stop bleeding. Not until the victim dies.

"'Is there anything that can change the dark silver back?' I asked.

"Seth told me that it is said a practitioner of white magic can lift the curse from dark silver. Even then, it's not guaranteed. Only the purest of hearts has a chance. It is the only thing his kind truly fears. That is the true secret of silver.

"The *drabarni* gave it to Seth. She carved the inscription into the handle. The dagger's blade isn't very sharp, except at the end. It's meant to stab. You pierce a werewolf with that blade, and nothing can prevent its death.

"Seth climbed back up the stairs. At the top, he looked down at me and said, 'Don't come up for anybody. Stay hidden until midday.' If he hadn't come back yet, I was to make my way to the sea. He told me not to go back to Castle Parlimae and to trust no one.

"I was terrified I would never see him again, so I called out, 'Seth? You be there tomorrow. Please don't disappear again. I couldn't bear it.'

"He nodded and shut the door over my head. I listened to the sounds of him leaving: heavy boots against the wooden floorboards of the church, the crack of his whip, and horse hooves pounding the earth as they rode into the forest. After he left, I took a closer look at the blade," mi Lady said, pulling the dagger from under her dress to show me. She had strapped it around her thigh.

The black blade shone like glass. The rosewood handle was carved in the shape of a cross. At the end of the handle was a blue sapphire. Across the guard was an inscription, Isaiah 40:29: "He giveth power to the faint; and to them that have no might he increaseth strength."

She pressed the dagger close to her chest for a moment, then slid it back under the strap around her leg. She stood back up and looked at the moon. When her gaze returned to me, her mouth was a solemn line, and I knew whatever she said next would be an unpleasant story.

"Later, Seth told me what had happened after he left," she said. "He rode hard to the edge of Mercel. As he got closer to the village, he could hear them. The wolves were howling wildly. Seth dismounted in the darkness just before town. He tied the buckskin to a tree. As he made his way to the town, he started the change.

"Like always, it started with pain. Every molecule in his body felt as if it were being pulled apart. It was searing, crushing, undeniable agony.

"His muscles moved and spasmed. The pores on his skin itched and then grew hair. Light fell over his brown fur, catching on the ribbons of black that wove around his massive arms, chest, and shoulders and giving them a bluish tint. These were the tattoos given to him by his Traveller family.

"Seth's eyes watered, and his breath became labored. Long, razor-sharp fangs stretched out from his jaw. His muzzle and ears stretched his skin as his eyes receded, leaving him with the extended snout and face of a beautiful wolf.

"His muscles became larger and more defined. His arms, shoulders, and chest expanded, tearing the shirt from his body. His thighs and calves grew with a more defined shape. A muscular half-man, half-wolf emerged. He stood nearly seven feet tall with his ears high and pointed.

"His hands and feet formed thick, powerful black claws. The last to change were his eyes. They became round orbs of brilliant, shiny blue. He was perfect, a creature of immense power.

"He moved through the shadows silently, his ears catching every sound. His hearing was far superior to that of a man. Within minutes, he was at the back of one of the houses on the edge of town.

"He could hear the wolves circling the livery. Remaining hidden in the shadows, he peered around the corner. There were five of them moving about. They were taking turns slamming against the barn, rattling and shaking the doors violently.

"The wolves were powerful, but the doors held. When the front door wouldn't give, they tried the rear. The pack kept watch on all of the exits, hoping to trick the occupants into thinking their attack at the rear meant the front entrance was clear for escape. They aimed to create enough fear to entice them to try.

"As Seth looked around, he couldn't see the black wolf. He could sense his presence. There was a faint musky odor in the air. William was there, all right, content to let his pack do most of the work.

"Seth could no longer wait. The doors looked like they were holding, but the wolves' impact was getting more violent. He was afraid the doors might shatter."

"Wait," I said, interrupting her. "You mean Seth is the one who saved Mercel? It was William—I mean, the black wolf—who was trying to break into the livery and kill everyone?"

"Yes," she said. "He couldn't risk the wolves crashing through the barn doors and chasing the townsfolk into the street. The moment the people were exposed, they would be slaughtered.

"He moved to the rear of the livery, careful to remain hidden behind buildings. As he got close, he watched the wolves loop back to the front door. One stayed behind to cover the rear. It wandered close to him, and he took his chance. With a mighty arm, he reached from around the corner and quickly grabbed the wolf.

"In one movement, he clasped a clawed hand over its muzzle and grasped its side with his other hand. He yanked the wolf into the darkness and quickly snapped its neck, killing it instantly.

"Seth slid the wolf quietly to the ground, careful to keep it behind the building and out of view of the other wolves. But they knew something had happened. They could sense his presence and smelled his scent in the air. As the pack pounded on the front of the barn, another wolf slowly walked toward Seth. Its nose was in the air, sniffing out Seth's scent.

"Seth silently reached up, pulling himself onto the roof of the barn. He watched as the wolf made its way down the alley toward the back of the livery, careful not to venture too close to the dark. It stopped at the corner of the building. It looked around nervously, sensing something wasn't right. It was too quiet, and his pack mate was not in position.

"He turned to look back at the front for just a second—another opportunity for Seth. He jumped from the roof and onto the wolf's back, breaking it. The only sound was the faint crunch of bone. The wolf's body smashed to the ground and went lifeless. Seth picked up the dead wolf and leaped into the shadows. He laid the body behind some lumber to the rear of a house, keeping it out of sight.

"A hideous howl wailed through the night air. Seth realized he hadn't been as stealthy as he'd thought. The howl made it clear that the black wolf had seen Seth kill two of his pack. He must have been watching the assault on the livery—probably saw Seth arrive too.

"The other wolves darted to the side of the building. When they saw their dead pack mate, they let out horrific howls, each yelling out in pain.

"Seth still couldn't see the black wolf, but now he knew he was there. He had to draw William out into the open. There was only one way.

"He leapt into the alley and faced the remaining three wolves. They snarled and snapped but did not advance. Seth stood there, slightly hunched and showing his large teeth. Saliva poured over his canines.

"The three wolves gained their composure. They were just about to attack when the sound of breaking glass filled the air. The black wolf jumped from the second story window of the building across the street. When he landed, his red eyes fixed on Seth. He was determined to kill him in that alley—that much was clear to Seth. William had missed his chance long ago and had blown it again when they fled Mercel two nights before.

"The three wolves looked back. With a slight movement of his head, the black wolf told them to charge. Seth readied himself for the attack. His clawed feet dug into the dirt as his hands drew into fists.

"The three wolves prowled toward him. They picked up their pace, trotting close enough to pounce. The lead wolf leaped for him, but Seth pivoted to the side and swung a mighty fist, catching the wolf in mid-air. The wolf let out a yelp as its body slammed against the livery wall.

"As it hit the ground, a second wolf ran toward him, its snout pulled back to reveal its long teeth. Seth caught the mouth in his hands. The wolf's momentum sent him reeling, and he fell to the ground. The wolf landed on top of him.

"He reached up with his other hand and pulled the wolf's jaws apart until its head snapped. He tossed the dead wolf aside as the third wolf jump at him. Blood sprayed from his forearm as its teeth sunk in.

"Seth swung his other clawed hand, striking the wolf across the side. Blood, fur, and flesh ripped from the creature's body. The blow sent the creature flying. It let out a cry of pain as it bounced off the ground a few feet away. The injured wolf scrambled to its feet and darted into the darkness.

"Seth climbed to his feet and took two steps toward the black wolf. He knew it was time to finish him. He exposed his fangs in a vicious snarl. The blue in his eyes became more intense.

"The black wolf stood motionless for a moment, stunned at the loss of his pack. Seth had killed them and barely suffered a scratch. It was not the moment the black wolf had hoped for, nor the outcome he had expected.

"The black wolf let out a frustrated howl, then darted down the street. Seth gave chase but was not fast enough. Within moments, the black wolf disappeared into the darkness of the forest.

"Seth realized he needed to get back to the church before William found me. The fight would have to wait. So he ran down an alley, behind some houses, and out of town. He was careful to hide in the shadows. By the time he reached the buckskin, his shape had returned to that of a man. He dressed in a coat and some spare clothes that he'd left with the horse, then raced back to the church.

"I had never left the secret room. He pulled open the door and came down the ladder. 'Did you kill him? William?' I asked by way of greeting. 'Is it over?'

"He shook his head and said, 'No. The townsfolk are safe. He slaughtered some of them. The rest managed to hide in the livery. I killed most of his pack, but he would not fight me. He ran off before I could catch him.'

"'Why won't he fight you? I thought you said he wasn't afraid of you,' I said.

"'He's not,' he told me. 'I think he wants you there. He wants to make you watch as he kills me.'

"I wrapped my arms around his neck and held on tightly. The thought was too much. I knew William could be cruel. There were times when we were children that he would act that way. But I never imagined the boy I knew could be so sadistic. I never imagined he could turn into this monster.

"Seth pulled back again. He said, 'I have to hunt him down. William cannot be allowed to form another pack.'

"He leaned back, looked into my eyes, and told me, 'Same plan as before. Wait until daylight, then make your way to the rocks by the sea. Hide in that cave just as we planned. I'll meet you there.'

"Then he went back up the ladder and shut the door again. That was the last I spoke to him. I was planning on staying there, but you found me before I was ready to leave. That's why we are not going to Castle Parlimae. Instead, we are making our way to the beach. He will find us."

By this time, the tears were flowing from her eyes. I knew she was afraid he might not make it to the beach. He had already fought William three times, two on this trip alone. And William was still out there. Now Seth was going after him again, trying to end this stretch of terror. But she had no way of knowing if he could win.

I didn't know if mi Lady realized it, but she not only had to worry about the black wolf but also the townsfolk. They blamed Seth for the murders in the valley that night. The woman saw Seth standing over the bodies, no black wolf in sight, and had assumed he'd killed them. And the man who had spotted the black wolf assumed he and Seth had killed those people together.

They didn't know Seth tried to stop the first murders. That he had defeated the pack and saved them. Or that it was he who had driven the black wolf from their town for the second time.

Worse, the woman had described the tattoos she'd seen on the creature in the alley. Anyone with those markings surely would be recognized as the beast. They would try to kill Seth the minute he entered the pub in human form. And Seth would not harm them, even in his own defense. This made him vulnerable. I hoped they didn't know the secret of silver, let alone dark silver.

And what about the Hessians? Where were they this whole time? Voelker knew the secret of silver, but did he know about dark silver? Regardless, he aimed to kill Seth as a werewolf or man.

It seemed everyone was looking to kill him. He would always be cursed, in more ways than one.

# TWELVE

# ALWAYS A MONSTER

er recounting of events took some time, though I was not sure how many minutes had passed. The horses had been done drinking for a little while. I had been consumed with what she was saying and didn't notice.

It was overwhelming. Most everyone knew the legend that said a werewolf's bite will turn you into a werewolf. Most had heard the story of a silver bullet killing a werewolf. I'd learned both growing up.

But I had never heard of dark silver, an element so evil that the worst creatures in the world cannot survive it. Black magic, were-wolves, William . . . It was a lot to take in.

I looked around the forest, digesting everything I had learned. A symphony of crickets filled the air. Frog song joined in. It seemed so loud in the silence of night, as if the animals were trying to see who could be the loudest.

The horses joined, adding their noisy breath to the cacophony. They were restless and exhaled in large, exaggerated puffs. They neighed a few times and stomped the ground with nervous energy.

I should have been just as nervous. William was still on the loose, after all. And we didn't know where Seth was. But I was enjoying the night. Until everything went silent.

The crickets stopped chirping, and there wasn't a frog to be heard. The horses stopped making noises momentarily as they looked around.

I could see the whites in their eyes. As their anxiety grew, they snorted and let out short grunts.

Mi Lady noticed it too. I stepped closer to her, and we both peered into the darkened trees. A shadow moved between them.

For some reason, mi Lady was not afraid. She took a few short steps toward the shadow. I turned and grabbed the musket from my seat. As the shadow got closer, she took a few more steps in its direction. Whatever it was, it had walked the tree line and onto the road. She ran toward the shadowy figure. It was Seth! He caught her as she jumped into his arms.

After a few moments, he led her by the hand back to the carriage. He was wearing only a coat and pants. The tattoos on his chest were visible under his jacket, impressive as they wove all over his upper body. The moonlight revealed the scars beneath the ink.

He looked at me and then scanned the area. He sniffed a few times. Something, a scent, was in the air. "We have to go," Seth said. "William is still out there. I lost his trai—"

Seth never got to finish his sentence. Out of nowhere, a black figure ran straight at us from the other side of the carriage. It hit Seth, knocking him to the ground with a loud thud. The impact was so powerful, mi Lady fell back a few feet. It startled me, too, and I fell backward, dropping the musket. Arca jumped straight up in the air, boxing his front legs.

It was the black wolf! He stood in front of Seth, between him and the carriage.

He turned back to look at me with a snarl. It looked like a smirk with those big teeth. As Seth was picking himself up, the black wolf turned back to him. Seth moved in front of mi Lady, blocking her from an attack. Her head peeked from behind his arm.

Seth took his jacket off and threw it to the side. Even in human form, he had a massive chest and broad shoulders. Every muscle in his body was flexed and ready for combat.

Without turning, Seth reached back and gently pushed mi Lady further behind. He needed to keep himself between the black wolf and her. But in order to defeat William, he was going to have to become something else.

Right in front of my eyes, Seth began the change. What she had described just a short while ago was now happening. And it was ugly.

He groaned under his breath. Those impressive muscles spasmed. They expanded and stretched, each becoming larger and more defined, which I hadn't thought was possible.

Hair began to cover his entire body. His head changed shape as his ears became longer and moved to their upper position. He opened his mouth in agony as his teeth grew. The incisors turned into fangs that extended like immense ivory spikes.

His muzzle elongated as his eyes receded. Within a matter of seconds, he had the head of a wolf. His eyes glowed that brilliant blue, their color exaggerated by the moonlight.

His right arm curled into a muscle as he lifted a clawed hand to the sky. With a clenched fist, he let out a terrible roar, completing the transformation.

I couldn't help but marvel at how magnificent he was: the beauty of his color, his perfectly formed muscles, the glow of his blue eyes, and the dark ribbons weaving in his fur. It was artwork.

I had seen him like this the night he battled the pack, but that had been in a much darker part of the forest. He'd been lit by the meager light of the coach's lamps. Here, with less tree cover to block the moonlight, I could truly see his power and beauty.

Mi Lady was right behind him. The look on her face said it was the first time she had seen him transform too. She might have been shocked to fear were it not for the black wolf, who was truly terrifying.

The black wolf was unfazed as his snarl grew larger. Slowly, he showed his own teeth as the weapons they were. Saliva dripped from his mouth like venom, forming two pools on the ground at his feet. It was as if he could barely wait for the fight to begin.

His hackles were on end. They looked like large black spikes fanning out above his neck. Even on all fours, he was just as muscular and impressive as Seth.

When he moved to circle Seth, I could see the striations in each muscle. He only seemed smaller because he was lower to the ground. From the looks of things, they were about the same size. Evenly matched.

The black wolf moved slowly as he attempted to get behind Seth. He was moving methodically, taking his time as he planted each foot. Neither beast wanted to make the first move. Both waited for the other to strike and make a mistake.

The horses were bucking and raising but they couldn't flee. I had set the coach's brake. The carriage lurched occasionally, but it was too heavy to move.

As the black wolf stepped in front of the horse team, he stopped. He looked back at me, and this time, his eyes shone red. This was a much more sinister look than the first.

In one fluid motion, he pivoted on his hind legs and clasped his teeth around Arca's neck. The horses went wild. Each bucked and pulled to break free. The beast's long fangs sunk deep into Arca's artery and severed it. Blood shot from the horse's neck.

I froze in complete shock. "NOOOO!" I yelled as I raised the musket, cocked the hammer, and fired. The bullet struck the black wolf square in the shoulder.

The beast let out a yelp but never let go of Arca. My horse died within moments. His body slumped to the ground. The weight of his one-ton body lay atop the harness and reins. Now the rest of the team wouldn't be able to move, even if I released the brake.

The black wolf got up, snarled, and let out a hideous cry. His teeth were fully exposed as he sounded his displeasure. It looked like he was about to leap at me, but Seth took a step, which drew his attention.

His head snapped in Seth's direction. The red in his eyes got more intense. There was a look of destruction set upon his face. This was complete, uncontrollable rage.

Seth and the black wolf stood motionless for several seconds. The black wolf gave a loud growl, and the sound got louder with each passing moment. Then both creatures sprang into the air.

Their bodies crashed together in midair, the sound loud in the silent forest. Their arms grappled. The black wolf bit down on Seth's shoulder as Seth snapped his jaws around the back of the black wolf's neck. His fangs sunk into the black wolf's muscle and skin. One of his clawed hands grasped the black wolf's throat, while the other dug into the wolf's back. His sharp claws sliced into the flesh like a knife through butter.

Tangled together in battle, they fell to the ground with a hard thud. The impact caused both creatures to let go and roll apart. They scrambled to their feet and began to circle each other again.

Blood dripped from their mouths along with saliva. Seth's claws were covered in both. While the wound on Seth's shoulder exposed muscle and flesh, Seth showed no signs of pain. The black wolf's wounds were deep. Blood oozed from the punctures in a steady stream. Both creatures moved as if they felt nothing, neither showing any weakness. They were as determined as ever to kill each other.

Without warning, they lunged at each other again. The black wolf raised on his hind legs, and Seth met him with force. Their teeth snapped as their heads banged together.

Seth leaned into the black wolf, the muscles in his thighs bulging with the effort. His claws dug into the black wolf's sides. They pierced the skin and slid into the muscle. The black wolf's claws tore at Seth's chest. He frantically bit at Seth, moving as fast as he could to inflict damage in as many places as possible.

As they were locked together in a veritable shoving match, mi Lady made her move, running back to the carriage. She came right beside me. Having reloaded, I raised the musket once again, cocked the hammer, and prepared to fire.

I knew it wouldn't kill him. My musket balls were lead, not silver, but they did hurt. If I got the chance, I was going to shoot the black wolf again. It might be enough of a distraction to help Seth kill him.

As they fought, Seth lost a few steps. He was losing his leverage and began to move backward. The black wolf sensed his advantage and gave one large thrust.

Seth pivoted to the side and swung his clenched fist at the black wolf's torso. The punch landed squarely against his rib cage. There was enough force in the blow to send the black wolf flying into the woods. He hit the ground and rolled into a tree.

Clearly stunned by the move, the black wolf struggled to his feet. Shaking his head violently, he tried to regain his composure. Seth stood on the road for a moment, his massive chest heaving as he took in air.

The black wolf walked slowly out of the shadowy forest. He crouched low to the ground. Seth's muscles twitched as he anticipated the creature's next move. He took a few steps backward, which prompted the black wolf to charge. He slammed into Seth, catching him in a backward motion. This rolled Seth right into the carriage, knocking the wind out of him.

Off balance, Seth struggled to his feet. He looked around at the driver's area of the coach. The black wolf leaped into the air, and Seth ripped the wooden brake from the carriage.

As the black wolf arched down, Seth jammed the stick into his side. A roar filled the air. Seth used the momentum to tumble the wolf to the side. What would have killed any other animal only enraged the black wolf.

He quickly got to his feet and grabbed the wooden spike with his teeth, yanking it out of his side. Blood squirted out, but the wound closed within seconds—the black wolf's healing power at work.

Without hesitation, the black wolf resumed the attack. He moved in on Seth, snapping and biting in a frenzied assault. Seth kept retreating, swatting the black wolf's muzzle away with each attempted bite.

Mi Lady and I fled from behind Seth, moving away from the carriage and into the forest. "We should run, mi Lady," I said.

"Where would we go? If Seth loses, William will run us down," she responded.

"We could cut one of the horses free," I said.

"We'll never make it. Seth has to defeat him," she said.

We crouched behind some trees to watch the battle. The longer it went on, the more enraged the black wolf became and the more intense his assault grew.

Frustrated that his frenzied attack was not working, the black wolf leaned back, preparing for another jump. As the wolf leaped forward, Seth grabbed the top rail of the coach and swung himself up. Instead of slamming into Seth, the black wolf landed behind him.

Seth scrambled to the front of the carriage to avoid the snapping jaws. When he was clear, he jumped toward the black wolf. As they collided, they rolled off the top of the carriage. The black wolf's back hit the ground, and Seth landed on top of him.

The black wolf kicked Seth in the midsection. The thrust sent Seth flying. He landed a few feet away, which allowed the black wolf to charge again. Stronger than before and with more force, he slammed into Seth, sending him flying into the tree that we hid behind. The impact shook the trunk and branches violently. For a few seconds, Seth lay dazed and motionless.

The battle was coming to an end. The black wolf was too much for him. Seth was losing strength. With each attack the black wolf made, Seth lost ground and became injured.

The black wolf charged again, ramming his head into Seth's chest and pinning him against an oak tree. This time, the black wolf didn't back away. He sensed the victory. He was savoring the moment.

As Seth leaned against the tree, exhausted and defeated, the black wolf moved within inches of his face. He taunted Seth with a menacing snarl. He wanted Seth to know he was about to die. His victory was all but assured.

A flash of crimson stole my attention: mi Lady's cloak. She dashed around the tree and thrust the dagger into the black wolf's heart! The night sounded of death: tearing flesh, breaking bones, and spurting blood.

There was a look of shock on his face. His mouth gaped, and his eyes went wide. Without so much as a whimper, the black wolf slid to the ground. The dagger of dark silver stuck out of his chest, firmly in place. The black wolf lifted his head and took a last look at mi Lady. She watched as the effects of the dark silver took hold.

The red glow in his eyes faded. His body shook violently. His ears and snout receded. His paws drew back into arms and hands. His tail disappeared, and his teeth returned to normal. Finally, his fur retracted to reveal the hairless skin of a human.

All that remained was a naked man covered in blood and gaping wounds. As I walked up, I could see it was William, the look of disbelief still on his face.

Seth pulled the dagger from William's chest. As he stood there holding the bloody knife, he began to change. His ears, muzzle, and teeth went back to normal. His eyes lost their glow, and his fur disappeared.

Mi Lady held onto him as he returned to a man. She tucked under his arm and stood with him as they stared at William's body. Seth looked at me and then back at the knife. "Dark silver," he said with a slight smile.

I looked back at the carriage, where the lifeless body of Arca lay. My heart was broken. I walked over to him and stroked his mane. But there was no time to mourn him now.

Seth was putting on his coat when the clip-clop of hooves rang through the forest. A slight glow, as if from lit torches, got closer and closer. People were coming—perhaps townsfolk from Mercel or Captain Barkslow. But a bad feeling sat in the pit of my stomach. It could be the Hessians.

No matter who approached, they wouldn't like finding William's naked corpse on the side of the road. And while Barkslow knew the truth, the townsfolk of Mercel would never believe the nobleman was some type of killer black wolf. If it was the Hessians, they wouldn't stop if they found out about Seth.

With Arca's body lying on the harness and reins, I couldn't move the team. There was just too much weight.

I ran to the rear of the coach, looking down the road. "Go," I yelled. "Unhook Killian. He's a good horse. Get to Port Calibre. I'll stall them, try to buy you enough time to get there and hide."

Seth and mi Lady moved toward me. "No," she said. "How are you going to explain this?"

"I'll be fine. They'll never believe I killed him. But if you are here, looking the way you do . . ."

"It's still William. They aren't going to like it," Seth said.

"I'll be fine. Go, before someone spots you," I said.

Mi Lady walked over and kissed my cheek softly. Both she and Seth were hesitant to leave me, but they turned and ran to Killian. Seth cut Killian's ties with the dagger before handing it back to mi Lady.

Once the horse was free, they hopped on his back and galloped off. Within a few moments, they were out of sight.

I watched them disappear, then turned to see the torches getting closer. The men's voices were clear and excited. They weren't going to like finding William dead on a desolate road. The manner in which he died was suspicious, which didn't bode well for me.

I summoned my courage. I needed to stall them long enough for Seth and mi Lady to get away. The longer I took, the more distance they could put between them and whoever approached.

Mi Lady wasn't wrong. I would have some explaining to do. If they didn't hang me first.

# THIRTEEN

# SOMETIMES LOVE ENDS JUST AS IT BEGINS

*T*jolted into action. As Killian carried Seth and mi Lady away, I cut Arca's straps. Once I got the doubletree free, I moved the second row toward the front. I finished with the last harness and climbed into the driver's seat. The group was on me before I had a chance to move.

Arca's dead body lay in the middle of the road, blocking half of the road. My carriage blocked the other half. A wagon full of villagers pulled up but couldn't squeeze past.

One man sat in the driver's seat; another sat beside him, holding a torch. The dozen men in the back carried torches, muskets, and plenty of ammunition.

"You're blocking the way. What's going on here?" the driver asked.

"My lead horse was killed. The second horse ran off," I said.

"Killed by what?" a man yelled out.

"I don't know. I stopped to take a leak and heard the commotion. I ran back and found him dead. I just strapped in the other horses and was about to go to the castle for help," I said.

"We're from Mercel," the driver replied. "Something or someone has been killing our people. We're on our way to the castle too."

I closed my eyes in disbelief.

"Lookie here," one of the men said, and my eyes shot open. "What's this then?"

He pointed to William's body. All heads turned to look. The man hadn't really been looking for a response, but I became instantly nervous and started to speak. "When I was coming down the road, I saw him there and stopped."

"I thought you said you stopped to take a leak," the driver said skeptically. The men gave me suspicious looks.

"Did you see anything?" the wagon driver asked.

"No. I was on my way, saw the body, hopped down. I went to take a leak, heard the raucousness, came running back, and found my dead horse. Whatever killed him must have killed my horse," I explained.

A couple of the men jumped down to take a closer look. They knelt beside William. "There is a hideous beast on the loose," one man said. "It kills everything it finds. This man is all torn up. It's the beast! Probably killed your horse too. C'mon, Let's get going."

Another man spoke up. "Wait a minute. I know this man. This is William from Castle Parlimae. How is he way out here in the Dark Forest all by himself? And where is his horse? Come to think of it, how did your second horse get out of his harness?"

Several more of the men jumped out of the wagon. This time, they yanked me off my seat. One of them pushed me up against a tree. "What the hell is going on here?" he snarled.

"Easy, fellas," I said. "I'm on your side."

"Side? What side? The Hessians told us there was some type of creature lurking about in these woods. Said it killed our people. They went after the damn thing but lost it."

"When did you see Colonel Voelker?" I asked.

"Yeah, that be his name—Voelker," one of the men said. "Saw him not long ago. Came to the town and rescued us. Said he's on his way to kill the beast."

"Voelker and the Hessians didn't save you," I said.

"What you mean? He opened up the livery and told us it was safe."

"This man attacked your town. William has been killing everyone around here," I said.

"Voelker said it was that stranger who killed the Tandeauxs a couple of nights ago. Didn't say nuttin' about William."

"Voelker's wrong." My words came out like a plea. "William is the black wolf. I was there that night. Seth was in the alley trying to stop the black wolf—William, I mean."

"Who's this Seth character you talkin' 'bout?" another man said.

"He's the one who came to the livery and rescued everyone. William killed the couple in the alley. Then he killed the grocer and his clerk. You all hid in the livery, and William's pack tried to break in. One of your boys found Seth at an abandoned church not far from Mercel. The boy told him what was happening. Seth came and killed the pack, then ran William off," I told them.

From the expressions on their faces, I could tell some of the men found my story hard to believe. But as they looked at William's bloody, ripped-up body, the truth started to sink in.

"Aye, it's true," one of the men said. "That is the way it happened all right."

"I thought you couldn't see anything from inside the barn," another man said.

"We couldn't, but when we came out, we found dead wolves near the livery. No idea how they died. What else could have done that?" the man said. "I was inside. I remember Sam talking to this carriage driver after the attack stopped. How would he know all of this unless he's telling the truth?"

"Where are the castle guards I left there?" I asked.

"They left after the Hessians came back. Said they were going back to the castle." The man thought for a moment. "If William is the black wolf and this Seth saved us from him, why is the colonel set to kill him?"

"What do you mean? Kill him how?" I asked.

"The Hessians went ahead to the sea. They told us to drive the forest and push the beast to them. The colonel's gonna kill him on the beach," the man said.

"We've got to stop him. Mi Lady is with him. They took the second horse and are trying to get out of here," I said, running back to my carriage and climbing up. "Take William back to the castle and tell Lord Parlimae to stop this. I'm going to the beach!"

A few of the men climbed onto the carriage with me. The others picked up William's body and loaded it into their wagon. They would go to Castle Parlimae to get some answers while we tried to stop Voelker from killing Seth.

The two horses could barely get the carriage moving. I couldn't push them too hard because Seth had yanked the brake off. I had no way to slow the carriage now.

We rolled along, and within a short time, we came to the split in the road. I hoped Seth and mi Lady had taken the route to the left, which went north to Castle Parlimae. If they had, I might be able to get ahead of them and reach Voelker before they did. With that thought, I snapped the reins and pushed the horses a little faster, guiding them down the road to the right.

We emerged from the forest moments behind Seth and mi Lady. I was shocked to see them racing through the open field and pulled the team to a stop. I thought I had bought them more time.

They continued past the field, following the road as it curved toward the sea. As they rounded the turn, Seth suddenly pulled the reins hard. Killian skidded to a stop, throwing sand and dirt in front of him.

Five men emerged from the shadows, fanning out across the road. The moon's light bounced off their muskets. Each man swung his musket onto his shoulder and put Seth in his sight.

Seth turned Killian back around, but he couldn't flee through the forest. A glow of torches shone through the woods, and it was getting brighter. More men. With the road blocked ahead and a mob to the rear, Seth turned Killian onto the beach.

He rode south, staying just beyond the rocks and avoiding the men on the road. As Killian raced on, a few more men emerged from the rocks in front of the horse.

A shot rang out. Killian dropped on his side, dumping Seth and mi Lady onto the sand. Seth was already starting to change when he hit the ground. By the time he stood back up, he had completely transformed into a werewolf. Saliva dripped from his mouth, and his tattoos glowed that strange blue again.

His towering frame stood over Killian's body. He looked down at the dead horse and let out a menacing growl. He bared his teeth violently at the men who shot Killian. They all took a step back. From the fearful disbelief on their faces, it was clear none of them had seen anything like him before. They trembled at his immense size.

His eyes shone with hatred for the men who'd killed the horse. The muscles in his body tensed, readying for a fight. Even wounded, he was a fierce creature to behold.

Mi Lady got to her feet and ran in front of Seth. She pulled the dagger of dark silver from under her dress. The men had reloaded and raised their muskets. They intended to fire again, but she stood before Seth and wielded the dagger.

His large arm curled around her, and he began to pull her to the side. But she wiggled out of his grip and remained in front of him. She knew they wouldn't fire with her in the way.

I wanted to believe he could get away if she stayed between them, but there was nowhere for him to go. He was cut off from any escape in all directions, and more villagers and soldiers were closing in from every direction.

The men regained their composure and put Seth back in their sights. They advanced slowly. Seth became more agitated, and a low grumble emanated from his throat.

Mi Lady and Seth were in a tight spot, but she seemed to believe they could get free—until she saw Colonel Voelker. He stepped out from behind a big rock. The moment Seth saw him, he let out a hideous roar.

Voelker had been waiting to ambush Seth the entire time. He had positioned men all over. The Hessian leader had directed the town of Mercel to drive the creature through the forest and to this secluded spot.

He anticipated Seth's entrance on the beach. Counted on the mobs of torch-wielding villagers pushing him right into the trap.

There was a slight grin on his face. He had the beast right where he wanted him. Voelker was finally going to get his revenge and kill one of the creatures that plagued his nightmares. He pulled a silver musket ball from his vest pocket. Seth's eyes widened at the flash of silver. His snarl grew larger, defiant. Colonel Voelker's grin grew. He kept his eyes on Seth as he loaded the musket.

Seth slid mi Lady behind him, out of the line of fire. He knew the Hessian did not care if she was there. Voelker would kill anyone who got in the way.

Mi Lady tried to move back in front of him, but this time, Seth held her back. She grabbed him by the arm and tried to pull him away. But he would not budge. Now he had to stand in front of mi Lady to protect her.

I was still at the edge of the field, having pulled the team to a stop. The men who'd traveled with me jumped out and filtered around the carriage to watch Voelker's standoff with the beast.

A few of the Hessian soldiers assembled behind Voelker, and they weren't moving. They waited for their leader to take his shot.

Seth made himself as big as possible to shield mi Lady from the bullet. More townsfolk arrived— the men of Mercel who had tried to catch Seth and the black wolf after the murders in the alley. They raced up the beach from the other direction, aiming for Seth.

The villagers around me realized what was about to happen. They ran forward, yelling for Voelker to stop and trying to catch the attention of the other men from Mercel. But the villagers couldn't hear them and Voelker ignored their cries.

Time seemed to stand still as Voelker took aim. He was just about to pull the trigger when a white horse emerged from the forest. Everyone, including Seth, looked up the road. The horse was galloping hard, carrying Lord Parlimae. Captain Barkslow and a few of his guards were on horseback just behind him, keeping pace.

A moment later, Seth turned calmly back to Voelker. He was still defiant but not as menacing—almost as if he could accept his death as long as mi Lady was safe.

Colonel Voelker would not be deterred. He shrugged off the distractions, took aim, and pulled the trigger.

I saw every detail, as if life moved in slow motion: Voelker pulled the trigger. The hammer of the musket struck the flint. There was flash from the ignition of the powder. Smoke billowed out the front of the muzzle.

I watched the bullet travel out of Voelker's musket. I could see the hole it made through the smoke. The wake of the bullet was visible against the dark background of ocean waves.

I saw the moment the bullet entered Seth's body. The silver ball pierced his chest, tearing a hole through it. Blood spurted in every direction.

Everything else was in slow motion too: The Hessian soldiers raising their muskets and taking aim. The mob of musket-carrying men putting Seth in their sight.

Seth forcefully pushed mi Lady away, knocking her to the ground. She covered her head just as the Hessians and townsfolk fired. Their bullets struck Seth moments after Voelker's. Each strike jolted him, and he fell to his knees.

A moment later, mi Lady turned to witness the terrible sight. Seth's body was peppered with musket balls. Each had ripped through his flesh. But those musket balls weren't the problem. Voelker's silver ball was the only one that mattered. It had hit the mighty beast square in the chest and made its way to his heart.

I saw the air rush out of his lungs, a mist captured by the moonlight. His body reeled for a moment. A few big puffs, and then he fell. The impact of his body spewed sand around him. Seth landed on his back.

Mi Lady's mouth was screaming "No," but I couldn't hear anything. The world had gone silent when Voelker took aim. I hadn't heard the report of the musket. I hadn't heard the sound of Lord Parlimae yelling as his horse skidded to a stop at the side of the road.

There was still no sound. Mi Lady scrambled on all fours to his side. Her mouth opened in a scream, but I heard nothing.

Tears streamed from her eyes, soaking his fur. With a trembling hand, she touched the bullet hole in his chest. There were traces of silver around the entry wound.

His eyes met hers. He reached out and touched her cheek. She pressed his giant paw to her face. Even from my perch on the carriage, I could see him returning to human form.

The change happened quickly. Within seconds, she was holding his hand to her face. As a man, his injuries were more pronounced. The bullet holes didn't close this time. All of them remained open, even the wounds from the lead bullets. And there were dozens of those all over his body.

The worst was Voelker's shot to the heart. Blood streamed down his sides. Ribbons of silver mixed with the red.

I jumped down from the carriage and ran to them, the villagers right behind me. We stood over him and watched as he took strangled breaths. His tattoos glowed indigo blue again. I don't know if the others noticed—nobody spoke a word.

Seth's lips move as he spoke to mi Lady. She leaned in and put her ear to his mouth. She sat up and nodded to him. With that, his eyes closed. His arm dropped to his side, and the glowing blue tattoos faded to black as the last of his life force left his body.

Still holding his hand, she covered her face and screamed at the top of her lungs. Slowly, sound returned to me, the quiet broken by her anguished cry. It was the scream of a woman who had just watched the love of her life get shot to death as he protected her one last time.

Voelker slung the musket over his shoulder and walked up the beach to Seth's body. His men flanked him on either side. Lord Parlimae and Barkslow made their way to the beach too. They pushed through excitedly but stopped short when they saw Seth.

I squeezed past a bunch of men and fell to my knees in the sand beside mi Lady. She laid Seth's hand across his chest. Then she looked over at me. The pain in her eyes was unbearable.

I looked up at the villagers and saw Voelker standing among them. His grin was gone. The look on his face was not what I had expected. He may have felt justified in killing the creature, but as he looked at the man lying dead on the beach, he seemed sorrowful.

Without a word, he turned and walked away from the group, his men right behind him. There was no celebration, no smiling, no sense of accomplishment. No pride for what they had just done. They quietly got on their horses and rode away.

As we watched them leave, Lord Parlimae put a kind hand on mi Lady's shoulder. "I'm sorry," he said softly. "This was not meant to be."

I didn't say anything, but resentment swelled inside me. I pushed past Lord Parlimae to help get mi Lady onto her feet. Together we walked from the crowd. The townsfolk moved aside as we came through.

Lord Parlimae ordered the men to wrap Seth's body in some blankets then carry him to our carriage. As they were placing him inside, mi Lady fell to her knees. Her screams of anguish were deafening. The agony filled the air.

Nobody knew how to react. Lord Parlimae finally came over and tried to comfort her. "I am sorry, my child."

With tear-stained cheeks, she looked up and said, "He wanted to go back to the church. I need to take him there."

"What church, child?" Lord Parlimae asked.

"The abandoned church in the forest," she responded.

Lord Parlimae nodded, then said, "I am going back to the castle. I have to tend to my son. You may stay with us after you are done. I will have my guards escort you safely to Trevordeaux when you are ready."

Mi Lady got to her feet. She collected herself, then started to climb atop the driver's seat of the carriage. Lord Parlimae helped her up while I latched the coach door and then climbed up the other side.

As I was just about to snap the reins, we heard the low rumble of wagons coming down the road. Making its way through the forest was a Traveller caravan. Their wagons had vibrant colors and ornate carpentry and were pulled by an assortment of painted ponies and speckled horses.

They rolled up to us and stopped in the grasses. The first wagon had two painted ponies pulling it along. A young man sat on the front porch, holding the reins. An older grey-haired man sitting beside him. If I had to guess, I would say these were the men who rescued Seth— his adoptive brother and father.

The next wagon was red with gold trim. An old woman steered two grey spotted ponies. Somehow, I knew this was the *drabarni*, the medicine woman who had healed him.

They were all there: The tattoo artist and the king. The dancing women and the card reader. More followed behind them.

The Travellers climbed down off their wagons. The men removed their hats and folded their arms. The women joined them, with the children clinging beside them. All wore somber looks.

The *drabarni* walked over to the carriage and looked at Seth's body inside. Her eyes lowered for a moment, then she stepped closer to mi Lady and looked up.

"We will take you to where he needs to go," she said. "Those who do not have a horse or wagon can ride with us."

Mi Lady nodded to her with a small smile. The *drabarni* made her way back to the wagon. The Travellers all got back in their wagons. They turned us west to make our way back to the abandoned church.

Lord Parlimae, Barkslow, and the guards rode back up the north road to return to the castle. Some of the villagers climbed aboard the Travellers' wagons, and then the caravan set off.

The procession was slow. The hour was getting late, and the moon was hidden behind dark clouds. So the Travellers lit torches to light the way through the forest. They spotted the hidden road much faster than I would have.

A slight fog hugged the ground. This made the church and cemetery look eerie as we came down the hill. When we reached the bottom, all wagons stopped in front of the church. Mi Lady jumped down and stood outside the coach, looking at Seth's body.

Women from the village and some of the Travellers came over and took his body. They carried him into the church, where he was cleaned for the ceremony. They cleaned the blood from his wounds with water and dressed him in fresh clothes—older garments of his that he'd stashed in the basement of the church ages ago.

Meanwhile, the Travellers were chopping down trees behind the church, where they'd erect a funeral pyre. The men constructed the pyre a few feet off the ground, right in front of the cemetery gate. They made sure it wasn't too close to the poisonous blackish red flowers that covered the gate.

Some men erected torches all around the cemetery so we could see. Others spread leftover oil from the church across the base of the pyre for easy lighting. And others built a wooden ramp that would allow all of us to pay our respects.

I helped Seth's adoptive father, brother, and a few others carry his body from the church. We placed him at the top of the pyre, under the stars.

We each took a turn walking past him to say a prayer for his soul, and ours. Some carried night flowers and laid them around his body. Others carried candles and place them around him.

Mi Lady was the last to view the body. She slowly walked up the ramp. She placed the dagger of dark silver into his hand. The black blade used to kill the black wolf shone under the light of the torches.

She folded Seth's arms across his body so the dagger rested on his chest. She made sure the inscription faced the sky. Then she leaned in and kissed his cheek.

I couldn't hear what she was saying, but I could read her lips. She whispered, "I love you." Tears fell from her cheeks as she returned down the ramp.

The Travellers brought over some clay cups for everyone, filling them with a bit of wine. As we raised our cups to Seth, one of Travellers played the fiddle and a young woman sang an old song. They later told me it was an old Scottish broadside ballad called "The Parting Glass."

Mi Lady used one of the torches to light the oil at the base of the ramp. She stepped back as the fire caught. In seconds, the entire structure was consumed.

Flames stretched high in the night sky, but none touched any of the trees. I saw a faint hint of blue on the edges of the flames. It was if they were guided by some magical force. I looked at the *drabarni*, who had closed her eyes. After a few seconds, she opened her eyes and raised her cup. "We honor him."

We all took a drink from our cups.

"You were the one he loved," the *drabarni* said to mi Lady. "He would take no other. He vowed to protect you always."

Mi Lady never said a word. She leaned down and gave the *drabarni* a warm hug. As she did, I saw the *drabarni* whisper something in mi Lady's ear. Mi Lady pulled back and nodded.

Not long after, the townsfolk departed. In a slow and methodical way, they rode up over the hill, returning to Mercel or the village at the foothills of the castle.

The Travellers got back into their wagons and started a slowly procession along the hidden road that climbed over the hill. They would disappear somewhere in the forest again. As dawn appeared, mi Lady went back into the church.

The *drabarni*'s wagon was last in the line. She held back, waiting beside her wagon. The caravan continued without her. It didn't take long until the Travellers were gone. She walked into the church, and I followed.

We found mi Lady sitting in the first pew of the sanctuary. Her eyes were on the cross at the altar. The *drabarni* sat in the pew beside her. Not wanting to intrude, I sat behind the *drabarni*.

"He loved you," the old woman said. "He loved you more than any other. He would serve anyone who needed him—it was his nature, the goodness in him trying to balance the evil cast upon him—but he loved you."

"I loved him too," said mi Lady in a soft, broken voice.

"We loved him, too, you know. I wish he could have remained with us. But it was not meant to be. The universe provides balance to all of us. Even to him. The black wolf could not exist without him, and he could not go on without the black wolf," the *drabarni* said.

Mi Lady looked at her with tear-filled eyes. "Do you mean that if I had not killed the black wolf, Seth would still be alive?"

"No, child," the *drabarni* said. "None of us knows what fate has in store. The black wolf had to die. He brought chaos to the world. To be in his shadow is bad luck. That is something to avoid.

"But the one we both loved, he was out of balance too. He was never meant to be part wolf. His destiny changed when he saved you. The evil of the black wolf spilled into him. This put him out of balance. Black magic has a way of doing this. It is like a disease: until the infection is purged, the body cannot heal.

"Dark Silver is man's attempt to restore balance. It's a way of combining something pure, like silver, with the wickedness of man to defeat evil. That's what you did."

Mi Lady looked at her. "Does it work?"

The *drabarni* smiled back. "He told you of the curse. And he gave you the blade. You tell me."

She looked up at the cross, then back at mi Lady. "But now you must finish making him whole again. Put things back in balance for him. That is your role."

Mi Lady's brow furrowed. "What am I to do?"

"You must tell him, child," said the *drabarni*.

Mi Lady looked taken back, as if the old woman had reached into her head and pulled out a secret. "How can I? He's gone."

The *drabarni* smiled again and stood. She reached out and kissed mi Lady's forehead. "Gone from this life. Not gone. Death is but another plane of existence. It is a beginning, not an end. The universe demands balance. He cannot truly rest until he has balance. Give that to him. Love him as he loved you."

I followed the *drabarni* out of the church. She got in her wagon and drove it up the hill. The wagon disappeared out of sight, headed in the same direction the caravan had gone.

When mi Lady finally came out of the church, she was wiping more tears from her eyes. She carried a satchel I hadn't noticed before, and I guessed the *drabarni* had given it to her. She walked over to what remained of the funeral pyre.

Seth's body was completely gone. All that remained were ashes. Mi Lady stooped down near the ashes, but I could not see what she was doing.

A few minutes later, she walked over to the carriage and opened the door. She looked at me for a moment. There was no smile, nothing but misery in her eyes. She spoke softly. "It's time to go."

# FOURTEEN

# THE SILENT ROAD

*A* day after the funeral, we left Castle Parlimae. Breakfast that morning was quiet and somber. Nobody was in good cheer. Mi Lady and I ate with Lord Parlimae and Barkslow.

I'd come to resent Lord Parlimae. He had ordered his men to capture, not kill, William. That was why they had been carrying shackles and silver-lined nets.

He could've stopped the bloodshed from the start, not only years ago but also recently. He had suspected Colonel Voelker's order from the king was a fake. But he couldn't risk confronting Voelker. Instead, he waited until Voelker found a reason to leave the castle before he acted.

I'd since learned that Lord Parlimae had planned to lock William in one of the catacombs under the castle. He would wait for Voelker to wipe out the rest of the pack, after which the Hessians would leave these lands. Voelker would never know William was the beast he was looking for, and William would no longer have a pack.

But Lord Parlimae's inaction gave William time to make his move. He couldn't kill mi Lady with Voelker around, so he attacked the farmer. He hoped that Voelker would hurry to hunt down the predator, believing it was close. And that's exactly what he did.

William knew mi Lady was looking for an opportunity to leave, so once Voelker and his men left the castle, he helped us escape. After all, if we were out in the open, he and his pack could come after us. And he'd get a chance to kill Seth, provided Voelker didn't get him first. Either way, he figured, he would have his revenge.

His was a newly revived thirst for Seth's blood. He'd spent years thinking Seth was dead. Seth had remained with the Travellers even after William butchered his family, keeping himself a secret. When he saw Seth in that alley in Mercel, William finally learned the truth.

He'd tried to kill Seth there, and he'd tried to kill mi Lady too. He chased vengeance again when we fled Mercel, dropping the tree to stop the carriage. The plan was simple: his pack would kill me, leaving William to deal with mi Lady.

But Seth showed up and defeated his pack, prevented him from hurting us. He had sulked his way back to the castle. As luck would have it, we showed up there later that night. But mi Lady was protected there, so he had to find a way to get her out in the open. The poor farmer paid the price.

Lord Parlimae knew of all the atrocities William had committed—all the murders in Mercel, in the valley. All the carnage and suffering he had caused. Lord Parlimae had done nothing to stop him.

Maybe it wasn't completely Lord Parlimae's fault. There wasn't much that could stop William anyway. Lord Parlimae knew the secret of silver, but it would've been hard for him to kill his own child.

Yet I struggled to understand how he could just look the other way, especially after William killed Seth's family. And to burn down the village to hide the crime . . .

He'd also learned Seth was still alive. Before I rode to the beach, I had told the men from Mercel the whole story. Some had taken William's body back to the castle. They encountered Lord Parlimae along the way and told him everything. Yes, Lord Parlimae tried to reach Colonel Voelker. But he was too late.

As mi Lady and I were about to depart the castle to finish our journey to Trevordeaux, Lord Parlimae and Barkslow walked out to the carriage. The lord opened the door for mi Lady.

"I'm sorry about William, my lord," she said.

Lord Parlimae looked away as he spoke. "He was my son. My only child. But what he had become was not him." He paused, then looked back at mi Lady. "I'm sorry for your loss. Seth was a good boy. He became a better man. When I find Colonel Voelker, he shall pay for what he has done."

Mi Lady looked at him with compassion. Nothing could excuse the fact that he'd allowed William to kill or that he'd covered up those crimes, but she had sympathy for the man. And perhaps our journey had forged enough of a friendship between us that I could read her emotions because I knew she was thinking that she never would have killed Seth, despite what he had become.

She gave Lord Parlimae a big hug. After all, he hadn't hired the Hessians. Even in my resentment, I understood: he was still a grieving father. Mi Lady always carried herself. She may not have been born of noble birth, but she was no less a lady.

"I'll send some of my men back to the cemetery and have what is left of his remains buried in a plot there. My mason will carve a stone for him." Lord Parlimae said with a deep breath.

He kissed her cheek and wished her well. Then closed the door behind her once she was inside. Looking up at me, he said, "Are you sure you don't want any of my guards to escort you to Trevordeaux?"

"No," I responded, looking out over the drawbridge across the valley. "I think it's safe now. There aren't any more of . . . them," I said with a wince. It was a little insensitive of me, considering his son was one of "them."

He never flinched. "Take care of her. Safe travels. I'll send for the extra horses after you arrive back at your company."

I nodded and tipped my hat to him. We pulled out, heading toward the main gate. As I turned, Lord Parlimae and Barkslow were ascending the castle stairs. Just before they went inside, Barkslow stopped and watched us depart. I thought I saw a flash of amber in his eyes. It was quick and then gone. I squinted, studying him more intently, but there was nothing.

*What the . . . It can't be*, I thought. But it was like seeing Seth's blue eyes in the forest when I first picked up mi Lady: a quick flash and then gone.

Barkslow grinned and waved. I raised my hand hesitantly as he disappeared inside the castle. The door closed with a loud bang behind him. Was this my imagination, paranoia, or something else?

I didn't know what to think. But I didn't have any fear at the moment, so I just shrugged it off. I quickly forgot about him as we made our way across the drawbridge and through the village. We continued along the road that cut between the fields, heading east until we reached the forest again. After half a day's ride, we made it to the seaside beach where Seth was killed.

It was different somehow. The sun was shining high in the sky, but that wasn't why the beach felt off. There was a subdued aura about the place now. We weren't in a rush, but we didn't stop either. Neither of us wanted to relive that night. If there had been another road, I would have taken it.

We made our way past the beachfront and continued on to Port Calibre. We reached the port in late afternoon and stopped. This was the last real town along the way.

I watered the horses and got them some oats at the livery in town. Mi Lady took a walk down to the water and watched the ships come in. Normally, I would have been a little more protective, but I could keep an eye on her because the livery was next to the seaport.

As I watched her walk toward the docks, I remembered the first time I saw her take a stroll. We had just come through the forest to stop in a clearing. She walked out into the field with such confidence, pride, and happiness.

Now, it was as if she was lost. She was only stretching her legs. There was no joy in her movements.

The horses were fine for the moment, so I walked out to join her. "You OK, mi Lady?" I asked.

She gave me a small smile, her gaze following the movement of the water. Her eyes were bright even if they were sad.

"Yes. I'm OK," she said.

"Mi Lady, can I ask you something?"

She looked over at me. "Go ahead."

"I delayed the villagers as long as I could. What happened on the road? We caught up to you quickly," I said.

She looked down and then back out across the sea. I could see she was recalling that time on the road. The look on her face suggested it was a fond memory. "We rode hard and fast through the forest. After a while, Killian was starting to slow. Recognizing he was getting tired, Seth pulled the reins back and stopped.

"Seth slid down his side to let Killian catch his breath. When he hit the ground, he fell to one knee. Light-headed and weak, he was losing strength.

"I slipped off the horse quickly to catch him before he fell on his back. Seth was hunched over. The fight had taken its toll, and his ability to heal wasn't working. Blood still poured from his open wounds.

"I was very concerned. 'Why aren't you healing?' I asked him. 'I thought silver was the only thing that could harm you. None of the dark silver touched you.'

"Breathing heavily, Seth pointed to a log that was laying on the side of the road. Killian turned his head and watched as we stumbled toward it. The pain at Seth's side caused him to wince as I helped him sit.

"Seth watched as a stream of blood trickled down his arm. 'Werewolves like me,' he started, 'we still feel pain. We bleed and suffer but normally heal quickly. The more powerful you are, the quicker you heal, though it takes our strength. Silver on the skin burns, but it will heal when removed. But pure silver to the heart kills.

"'Attacks from another like us, those who have turned, can hurt us. We don't heal from those wounds like we do when wounded by a human. We can kill each other. That is why I was able to kill most of the pack in Mercel. It's also why I rarely carry any silver weapons. I only carried the dagger because it was a gift from the *drabarni*. It probably has something to do with the curse. Maybe it's the evil. We don't usually fight among ourselves so this is very rare.'

"With all that in mind, I wasted no time. I hurried over to Killian and plucked a hair from his tail. I washed it in a small stream that ran alongside the road, then I pulled a pin from my corset and washed it too.

"I went back to Seth and tied the hair to the pin. It wasn't exactly clean, but I didn't have any boiling water. It was the best I could do at that moment.

"A small ray of moonlight was peeking through the forest beside Seth. I nudged his arm into the light so I could see. I threaded the horse hair through his flesh, pulling it together. When the wound was tightly closed, I tied it off and cut the excess thread with my teeth.

"With the wound closed and the bleeding stopped, his tattoos glowed blue beneath the moon's rays. His flesh began to heal.

"I moved on to the next gash and closed it the same way. When I was done with that, I moved to the wound on his side, then his leg, until I'd stitched up each cut. Just like before, the wounds began to heal once the flesh had been sewn and the bleeding had stopped. Each time the healing process started, his tattoos shone blue.

"Seth sat patiently as I stitched him up. His breath slowed, and he began to relax. As he watched me tend to his injuries, his heart stopped racing.

"'You do good work,' he told me.

"I looked at him and smiled. It was a weak smile and one of worry. I knew we weren't out of danger yet, but the pack was gone, and the black wolf was dead, so I was safe. It was Seth who was in danger. Especially in his weakened state.

"The townsfolk of Mercel believed he was responsible for the murders. Witnesses saw him over the bodies back in the alley. They didn't know the truth. It was Seth, not the Hessians, who had chased William out of the alley. The Hessians merely followed the trail left behind.

"The black wolf and his pack had continued to terrorize the village, attempting to kill every one of them. They killed the shopkeeper and his assistant, leaving their bloodied and ripped-up corpses for everyone to see. Then they howled from the darkness to create more fear and panic.

"Most of the villagers stuck together. They managed to find safety in the livery. Had Seth not arrived, the pack would have broken down the doors and killed everybody. It was Seth who had saved them. But nobody saw any of that.

"Lord Parlimae had Barkslow and his men looking for William. Sooner or later, they were going to find his body, naked and torn to shreds on the side of a road deep in the forest. Lord Parlimae knew the truth, but it's hard to predict what a grieving father will do. Would he be looking for the one responsible? Looking to avenge his son's death?

"He had no way of knowing I was the one who actually killed William. Seth was going to get blamed for that too. And I figured Lord Parlimae wouldn't want anyone knowing the truth about William.

"Plus, the Hessians were out there somewhere. After William attacked the farmer to draw me out of the castle, Colonel Voelker and his men had left to hunt the creature responsible. Nobody has seen or heard from them in some time. The forest was big, but I knew they wouldn't leave the valley. Voelker and his men were experienced hunters. And they were not the type of men to give up.

"As I looked at Seth's battered body, I wondered how we were going to make it through the night. He had suffered so much for me already. He'd protected me all of my life, even from afar. Even when I didn't know he was there, or that he was alive. In the past three days alone, he'd fought devastating battles that would have killed an ordinary man. I didn't want to lose him again.

"Seth stood and reached out to me, pulling me up. He looked at me like nobody had before, at least not for a long time. His eyes were soft and tender. The blue in his irises sparkled in the moon's light once again. When he looked at me like that, it was hard to catch my breath.

"My heart was beating so fast, a swift but steady rhythm. It was like a drum. Our eyes met, and I could see the love in him.

"He reached out and touched my face, brushing my hair aside. I closed my eyes. It felt as if an electric current flowed through me, just like when we were teens. It sent chills down the back of my neck and raised goosebumps on my skin.

"I felt flush and warm as he caressed my face. I could barely hold a thought. They all ran together in a mix of emotions I had not felt in years. It was hard to catch my breath.

"He leaned forward and slowly kissed my lips. It was soft and tender at first. His hand moved up through my hair as he pulled my head closer to him, and the kiss became more intense. Then he leaned in with his whole body, pulling me close. I could feel his warmth and strength as he pressed against me.

"His other hand slipped down to my lower back. Suddenly, he broke the kiss. He turned to look down the road behind us. I stopped and listened intently but could neither see nor hear anything.

"Seth's chest became full. His arms drew back, and his stare intensified. He reached for my hand. We have to go. They're coming, he told me.

"He took me by the hand and ran to Killian. In one motion, he swung a leg up over the horse's back. Then he reached down and pulled me up behind him. Once we were both ready, he snapped the reins and kicked the horse in the side.

"Killian bolted down the road. I looked back but couldn't see much through the cloud of dust that followed in our wake. But there seemed to be a faint glow coming in the distance.

"At that point, I knew it was the villagers. I didn't know what had happened to you, but I assumed it wasn't good. That is when we emptied out onto the beach and all hell broke loose."

When mi Lady finished her tale, she looked back at the water. Sadness returned to her face. Her eyes lost their sparkle as we returned to the carriage.

She sat inside the coach, cloaked in shadows, and waited. She didn't have to say anything; I knew she wanted to go now. I finished with the horses, climbed back up into the driver's seat, and got us going again.

We left Port Calibre on the road that headed east. As we left the sea, the path took us into the forest. The smell of salt water and fish started to fade. This was the last leg of our journey. Our next stop would be Trevordeaux.

Daylight gave way to night. This part of the forest was filled with small- and medium-sized rocks. Moonlight fell over the moss that covered each rock. It was a beautiful thing to see.

The forest wasn't as scary anymore. The sounds of night became melodic and soothing. Crickets filled the air with their constant chirping. And the frogs' throaty song carried through the trees. The sound was so loud in some parts, I figured there were a million of them.

We drove all through the night. Occasionally, I stopped to give the horses a rest. I petted them and gave them more oats. This gave them energy and kept them happy. It was nice, but I just didn't bond with them like I had with Arca and Killian.

During stops, mi Lady never got out of the carriage. I checked on her through the windows and found her in the same position: sitting up and gazing out the window—not at anything in particular. Hers was an empty stare.

We drove through the night and into the next day. The dawn came slowly, bringing with it shades of purple and pink. It had been a long ride from Port Calibre, but we finally broke free of the forest.

This was open country, full of tall grasses and wide meadows, rolling hills and little streams. Occasionally, I spotted a small pond in the low places. This was a big difference from the forest. I could see for miles on end.

As we got closer to the city, the grassland turned into fields with crops. We passed herds of cows and flocks of sheep. Peasants tilled the land, which they rented from the wealthy lords and nobles of Trevordeaux.

This road continued east, moving slightly north. Far off in the distance, past these fields and the forest that abutted them, were tall peaks. Their snow-covered peaks melted beneath the last of the fall sun.

By the end of that day, we reached the city of Trevordeaux. It was big and bustling, with a river running from the mountains through the middle and eventually to the sea. The city was a major trade route, connecting our country to the many lands of the east.

When we got closer, I could see more roads leading in and out of the city. There were plenty of travelers now too. On our journey, we hadn't passed a lot of other carriages. There were a few riders on horseback and some farmers in the fields, but the Dark Forest was a lonely place. Like most cities, Trevordeaux had carriages on every street.

We entered from the west side of town. The wealthy inhabitants lived here, and they all had a horse and buggy.

I glimpsed three or four carriage companies, each providing transportation to citizens who did not wish to walk across the city. Those who didn't want to walk but didn't have a carriage were on horseback. Everything was proper on this side of town: men wore tricornes and women wore bonnets. Those on foot didn't just walk; they strolled.

The street we followed went through the center of the city. A few blocks in, we came to a large park. I steered the carriage around it, careful not to hit any pedestrians who were crossing.

The city government building was here, along with a big library and several uptown markets. This was the cultural epicenter. The biggest church in town was on the corner as well.

After we maneuvered around the square, we followed the street to a river. The carriage rolled north alongside the river for several blocks.

The river didn't sit idle. It was a highway of commerce. Boats were carrying cargo upriver from the sea. Some dock workers were unloading ships' hauls, while others were filling ships with goods from Trevordeaux.

We moved north on River Street. Horses' hooves and carriage wheels clattered over the cobblestones. Merchants were ending their day. Sidewalk vendors were packing up for the night, and every now and then one stopped sweeping long enough to watch us go by.

A few blocks later, we came to the stone bridge that connected to the east side of the city. The area was home to the peasantry, including mi Lady's grandmother.

I crossed the bridge, spotting a tavern on the corner. *I could really use a drink right about now*, I thought. The sound of music and festivities rang out from inside. Neighborhood folk came and went through the front door.

This section of the city was a little different from the West Side. Here, there were rows of sod houses with thatched roofs. They were tightly packed together and went all the way to the Great Eastern Forest that bordered the eastern edge of the city.

These were the homes of the farmers, the dock workers, and laborers for the wealthy who lived on the West Side. It was a working-class community.

Children played in the streets while parents tended large gardens. Many homes had small barns in the back yard. Chickens and other livestock grazed and meandered about.

As the horses clomped down the street, I scanned my surroundings, intent on taking in the city. I could smell freshly cut flowers from local shops. Pigs hung in the window of a butcher shop that had closed for the day. Further down the street, I passed vegetable and fruit markets, which supplied fresh produce to the neighborhood.

I saw a livery at the end of the road. There were several horses tied to posts out front. A farrier was putting shoes on a few of them. A stable boy was hauling bales of hay inside for the evening.

The Great Eastern Forest started right behind the livery. It followed the curve of a tall hill that overlooked the east. Its dark trees seemed to touch the sky. The forest went on through several different countries, eventually leading into the lands of Wallachia.

I turned the carriage north, putting the river on our left. This road would continue through more farmland until it reached the mountains. Mi Lady had directed me to continue for a few blocks. Her grandmother's house was near the end of the city, just before the sheep farms.

We continued until we reached a house near the end of the road. It was a quaint little home—not expensive but well-kept and neat. Purple flower boxes sat in every window. A small, gated fence enclosed the yard.

Several buggies were parked on the street in front of the house. A small crowd of men and women gathered on the porch, all of whom were dressed in black. They watched our approach intently.

I pulled up to the front and stopped. Not only had Lord Parlimae supplied us with two additional horses to replace Arca and Killian, but he'd also asked his men to fix the brake. I set it, then hopped down from the driver's seat. I opened the carriage door.

Mi Lady stepped out, wearing her red cape. Lord Parlimae had had it washed and pressed. Her hood was up, and she was carrying a handkerchief.

I pulled her bag from the roof, then ran over and opened the gate for her. She paused just before she went through, gathering herself. Her head lifted, shoulders pulled back, and posture straightened.

She strolled through the gate with pride and confidence. I knew she was in pain, but I was the only one who knew why. I shut the gate behind me and carried her bag to the front porch.

Friends and relatives greeted her with smiles and hugs. They shared news mi Lady had no doubt dreaded, especially after losing Seth: her grandmother's condition had worsened. They had come to say their goodbyes.

Nobody noticed me as I set her bag down, so I headed for the carriage without a word. There was so much I would have liked to have said, but it seemed pointless now.

As I looked back at the house, mi Lady turned her head to me. Our eyes met for a moment. She looked to the ground as a tear fell.

I knew she was close to her grandmother and was saddened by her illness. But her grandmother was a still alive, and mi Lady would be able to spend some time with her. That tear hadn't been for her grandmother. She mourned for somebody else.

I nodded and smiled to her, then walked back to the carriage and climbed into the driver's seat. Like I had done so many times on this trip, I snapped the reins to get us going.

As the carriage rolled past the house, I glanced through a window. An elderly woman lay in a bed with a blanket pulled up to her chin. When mi Lady walked through the door, the woman smiled. Mi Lady removed her hood and sat at the edge of the bed. She leaned down and gave her grandmother a hug and kiss on the check. She held her grandmother's hand as they spoke for the first time in many years.

The carriage rolled passed the window until I could no longer see. I knew I could leave now, as I was no longer needed. She was finally where she needed to be. But I felt empty inside.

I was glad to get her to her grandmother's house. Glad she was able to spend even a little bit of time with a person she truly loved before it was too late. I was even glad she'd had time with Seth, however short it was. But I was sad to leave her behind.

The entire journey weighed heavily on my soul. I left the city, continuing north. I had no intention of going back through the Dark Forest. My map showed that this road ran through the mountains and connected to a road on the other side, which would take me back to my city.

The mountain pass was even colder than the forest had been. And the ride was slow—it took me nearly two weeks to reach home. My city wasn't as big as Trevordeaux, but it was a welcome sight.

I went straight to the company livery. The moment I pulled in, my employer came over to greet me. I got the sense he'd been waiting. I was several days overdue, and he was nervous. He was less concerned for me than the company property.

Stories of a carriage running into trouble in the Dark Forest had already reached his ears. Some of them were absurd. Others were pretty close to the truth. But not one mentioned a werewolf.

My employer wanted to know every detail. I tried to explain as best I could, but it just didn't come out right. Nothing I said made a lot of sense.

When he saw that Arca and Killian were not with me, I was forced to tell him they were dead. It would have been hard to explain that a giant black wolf killed one horse, and men trying to kill a werewolf shot the other. So I lied and said they died from a disease that spread through the valley. That was sort of true.

He really didn't care why they had died. The company would have to return the horses Lord Parlimae had loaned me. So not only would he lose the replacement horses, but he'd also need to find somebody to take them back before a lord caused him issues.

Then he looked at all the damage to the carriage. Scratches from the black wolf marred the doors. Seth's blood spotted the interior. Fortunately, the red velour hid the bloodstains, so I didn't have to answer for that one.

His gaze climbed to the brake. Though Lord Parlimae's men had replaced it after Seth tore it off, the handle didn't match the carriage. And it was really noticeable.

He came to the conclusion that I'd lost control of the carriage and gotten the horses killed. As far as he was concerned, I never should have gone through the wild country.

I laughed. I reminded him that I'd chosen that road because he had ordered me to take the most direct route. I also pointed out that he'd told me to stop in Mercel. That he gave me all the information on the place. That he made the reservations for us at the inn.

But my employer would hear none of it. He said I had a bad attitude, and it was my responsibility to take care of company property. He fired me and kept my pay as compensation for the damage. Then he ordered me to get my things and get out.

Losing my job really didn't bother me. In some ways, I was relieved. At least nobody was going to ask me to travel through a dark forest anytime soon. I grabbed my musket from the driver's seat, gathered what little stuff I had from my quarters, and cleared out.

Holding a job was hard when you were chased by rumors and plagued by nightmares.

Word traveled fast in the courier business. Losing horses of Arca and Killian's quality was a career killer.

So I packed up and set out for somewhere else. I moved from city to city, staying to the northern part of our country. I avoided the areas to the south, especially places near the Dark Forest.

There were always jobs cleaning stables. They never paid that well, but I earned enough for a place to stay and something to eat. If the work was good, I had enough to drink.

For a long time, I suffered from nightmares. Sleep was hard to come by, so I used my supper money to buy ale that would send me to sleep. And if it was a really good week, I'd have coin for the harder spirits.

But insomnia became an excuse, and my drinking got worse. It was always the same: I would enter a town and get a job working the stables or some rich folks' farm. I especially liked it when they gave me a bunk in the barn. The less I had to spend on lodging, the more money I had for ale.

It didn't take long for me to get fired, again and again. It was hard to keep a job when I was drunk all the time. But it was the only thing that numbed the pain.

As the months passed, the memories of my journey through the Dark Forest began to fade. The bodies in the alley, the black wolf, the pack, a werewolf—eventually, it all felt like a story, not something I'd lived through.

There had been the pleasant moments of the ride, and I tried to remember them even as I worked to forget the horrors.

Mostly, I thought of her. When I closed my eyes, I smelled the perfume she wore that first night. It'd been a hauntingly sweet aroma.

Sometimes I thought back on the night we met: The way she had glided down the steps of her mansion. How her cape had flowed dramatically behind her as she walked. The manner in which she'd strolled through the moonlit meadow, skimming her fingers across the flowers.

No, I would never forget her. Nor would I forget what we lived through or the story she told.

# FIFTEEN

# ONLY LOVE
# DEFEATS EVIL

I took a gulp of ale, then set my mug down. It was empty, and I needed another. I raised my finger to get more, and a wide-eyed boy flipped a coin on the bar. The barkeep ran over and filled my mug without hesitation.

Quite a crowd had formed around me. There must have been fifteen men and women hanging on my every word. I was half in the bag already, and it was barely past suppertime, but I could still weave a tale.

It must have been the millionth time I'd repeated this story. I could recite it in my sleep, if I could sleep.

The bar was silent while I told the story. I'd learned to become more animated as I talked. It became a performance of sorts, a way to keep people engaged—and happy enough to buy me another ale.

I liked this pub, even though it made me a little nervous to be this close to the Dark Forest. The patrons seemed to be a little more willing to accept what I was telling them than folks I'd met in other parts of the country. Maybe that was because Port Calibre was a sea town. Fishermen told tall tales all the time.

That the region was part of the story's setting might've made them more likely to believe too. My story was probably something they'd already heard, to one degree or another. The only difference: I was a firsthand witness. The real question was whether they believed me.

There were all kinds huddled around me. Fishermen in black hats filled the bar with smoke from their pipes and scented the air with different aromas. Apple and cherry were my favorites.

Bar wenches in frilly tops poured ale and whiskey. Barflies swigged mugs of ale. Ruffians—some of whom looked like highwaymen—kept to the shadows but sat close enough to hear my tale in case there was an opportunity in it.

I spotted a few sailors from the military vessels in the harbor. There were soldiers from various armies too—allies of the French being transported by ship to various locations around the globe. I even noticed a few well-to-do aristocrats and nobleman hanging around to hear my account.

The more I spoke, the more intently they all listened. Each of them leaned in and stayed quiet. When people talked or made a noise, the crowd shushed them. Nobody wanted to miss anything.

As for the story, nothing was off limits. I told the entire story. Listeners always loved the parts about the werewolf. The women in particular liked hearing of mi Lady and Seth. They seemed to swoon a bit when I described their first encounter after the attack on the road from Mercel.

I told this story in every pub I came across, reading the crowd and adjusting the account as needed. Sometimes I embellished events. Other times, I left out details I thought they wouldn't buy. No matter where I told the story or how I changed it, the end always left them choked up.

This crowd was no different. The women cried, using handkerchiefs to wipe their eyes. Some of the men tried to hide their tears by pretending to blow their noses.

I finished the last of part of my tale and waited for someone to buy me another round. An old-timer seated close to me raised an eyebrow and pulled a cigar butt from his lips. He leaned in. "Hogwash. Pure hogwash, I say."

He laughed ridiculously. An old woman slapped him on the back and let out a thunderous laugh of her own. "Very entertaining though. I'll give you that. Very entertaining. I haven't heard one like that in years."

"Werewolves, Lord Parlimae's son being one of them." She shook her head. "Very entertaining indeed."

They both finished laughing and took big gulps from their mugs. I looked around and saw many faces smiling, but nobody offered to buy me another round. That was always the problem with the end of a tale. People bought me ale to entice me into telling a story. They continued to buy me drinks so I would finish the account. But they only bought me drinks at the end of a story if they really like it.

I had thought they believed me, but apparently they didn't. Not all of them anyway. To them, I was just another drunk in a bar telling a tall tale that was entertaining enough to pass the time. Even the young boy who had bought me the last round smirked and left.

Out of money and with no one offering to buy me another drink, I made my way to the door. The worst part was, I was only half in the bag. I was going to need a hell of a lot more ale if I wanted to fall asleep.

It was cold outside. I pulled my jacket collar up around my neck. Streetlamps provided plenty of light in the darkness of night. The moon was full and would guide my way back to the livery. It reminded me of the moon from many months ago. The biggest difference was that it didn't give me the creeps. Enough time had passed that I was no longer afraid or sad when I saw a moon like this.

I made it back to the livery and went inside. Most of the horses were resting quietly. I didn't have a room in town, so I would probably bed down in one of the empty stalls. But I wasn't ready to sleep right now. Instead, I went out the back and stood next to the corral.

Sometimes the farrier would let a few horses out on a clear night. I liked to feed them and scratch their noses. I couldn't drive a team anymore—nobody had any use for a drunk carriage driver, never mind one who'd lost two horses and damaged his coach—but it made me feel better to be around them.

As I stood there, petting a gentle mare, a sweet, subtle aroma made its way through the stables and to my nose. It was a familiar smell, one I had only encountered once before. The scent was the same as it had been the night I pulled up to the Duke of Harcourt's mansion.

A small, frail voice spoke from behind. "You told the tale well. Every word was true. Every word."

Her voice took my breath away. I knew exactly who it belonged to. I turned, eyes wide with anticipation.

A shadow peeled away from a patch of darkness next to the barn. The woman walked into the moon's light. She remained hidden beneath a long, dark green cloak with a cream lining. She reached up and lowered the hood. It was mi Lady.

She wore a pleasant smile, and her brown eyes glimmered. There was a softness about her face. Although it had been a number of months since I last saw her, she looked the same. I could still see the pain deep inside, but something about her was different. She was content now.

"Mi Lady, I thought never to see you again," I said humbly. "You heard?" I paused. "I didn't see you in the pub."

A wave of embarrassment came over me. I was a drunk, even if I wasn't completely drunk tonight. I had no place to call my own. Hell, I didn't even have a place to sleep tonight. I had no real purpose in life.

She reached out and put a hand on my shoulder. "They may not have believed it, but you and I both know the real story."

She paused and with a serious voice said, "I need one more favor of you."

My eyes looked up and met hers. She didn't have to say anything; I knew the favor she was asking for. I shook my head, a sense of fear rising in me. I searched for an excuse and finally landed on the truth. "Nobody will hire me to drive a team anymore, mi Lady. I'm sorry."

"Come with me," she said before turning to walk through the livery.

I followed her out to the street. Parked in front of the barn was the most magnificent carriage I had ever seen. It was black, like the one the black wolf had damaged, but much larger.

Four large lamps hung from each corner, their candles lighting up the night. The black paint shinned in their glow. The wheels were white with a black coating on the rims.

I couldn't help myself. I strode closer to inspect the interior. It was lined with white crushed velvet, and white curtains hung from the many windows. The seats were stuffed with goose feathers.

The carriage was harnessed to a six-horse team. Each horse was white as snow and had a long mane and matching tail. They stood proud and tall in their black harnesses. The lead horse looked over at me and neighed.

I walked up to him, reached out, and placed a hand on his snout. He was sure of himself and confident—definitely the leader of the team. He reminded me of Arca.

Turning to mi Lady, I said, "This carriage is fit for a princess or duchess. Is this your husband's?"

"No. And I am no princess. Neither am I the Duchess of Harcourt," she said.

"I don't understand," I stated.

"The Duke of Harcourt and I have parted ways. I never returned to Normandy. I have not seen that land since we left those many months ago. The duke and I agreed to dissolve our marriage," she said.

"I'm sorry, mi Lady," I responded.

"It's OK. Ours was a marriage of convenience. He wanted a young wife to establish himself with the crown. I needed to take care of my grandmother. At first, he was OK with the arrangement, but later he changed his mind," she said.

"Arrangement?" I asked.

My questions clearly made her uncomfortable. But I would need answers if I was to take her anywhere. She walked closer to me and stroked the lead horse's mane.

"You know that I cannot bear children," she said. I nodded. She'd said as much when she told me about her time with Seth. "My husband knew this when we married, but when he was named governor of Normandy, he changed his mind. He wanted children to carry his name. That last moment on the steps, when you picked me up, was our parting farewell. Did you never wonder why the trip was not a round trip?

"After my grandmother passed, I remained in her house, which is where I live now. It's nothing fancy. The place is quaint and humble, just like the house I grew up in at the foothills of Castle Parlimae.

"The duke provided me with a generous endowment. I used some of that to purchase this carriage, including this team. I also spent a little on a new cape." She looked over at me and smiled. "Was that wrong?"

I guess she was no longer a duchess or even a lady—at least not as the title would imply in polite society. No matter what, she would still be mi Lady to me. But now I had to confront her request.

"Where is it you want me to take you?" I asked even though I was pretty sure I knew the answer. I just didn't like it.

She looked back at me with a slight smile. "I need you to take me back. Back to where we both last saw him. The beach."

She walked over to the carriage door, looked over at me, and waited. I let out a heavy sigh, picked my head up, pulled my coat straight, and gathered myself. I walked over reluctantly.

"Mi Lady, before I take you back there, I need to know why you want to return after all these months. We were nearly killed, and lots of people died. Why are we going back?"

She gave me a triumphant smile. Only after I'd replayed my words did I understand her expression. I had asked why we were going back, implying I'd already decided to take her. She'd known my decision before I admitted it to myself.

"I need to tell Seth something I could not tell him before," she said. "When I was attacked as a girl, the day William knocked me off the mare as I rode through the fields, I wasn't ducking chores just to go riding. I was riding out to find Seth. To tell him."

"Tell him what?" I asked.

"What you must understand is that the three of us had been close when we were young. William, Seth, and I. As we got older, William started to show more signs of being cruel. He grew meaner. Enjoyed killing and hurting others.

"At first, I thought he was just a bully, that he'd grow out of it, but later I knew it was more. It was his nature. He and I grew further apart. As that happened, Seth and I grew closer. We would sneak away through the forest. The abandoned church was a favorite spot of ours. It was far away from everything and was usually empty and quiet.

"The day of the attack, I was on my way to find Seth so I could tell him I was with child. His child.

"When William attacked, he not only sliced my neck but threw me from the mare. The impact of the landing caused a lot of damage. The doctor tried to help, but I lost the baby. I never got a chance to tell Seth because I thought he had been killed. I was devastated. I lost both him and the baby that day.

"I couldn't tell anyone. When I found out Seth was alive, I planned to tell him. I wanted to tell him at the abandoned church. But once he had told me everything that had happened in his life, I couldn't bring myself to do it. Seth had been determined to rescue the townsfolk in Mercel. If I had told him about the baby, resentment, rage, and revenge would have consumed him. I was afraid it would get him killed.

"I wanted to tell him after he returned, but he left again to kill William, and there wasn't time. When he caught up with us on the road, William appeared before we had a chance to talk. Everything happened so fast. There just wasn't time.

"After Voelker shot him, when Seth was dying on the beach, he asked me to take him home. He wanted to be buried at the cemetery, behind the red door." She had not mentioned a red door before—nor had I seen one—but it didn't seem like the right time to ask while she was discussing one of the worst days of her life. For now, I listened.

"At the funeral, the *drabarni* told me of the Travellers' belief in the balance of life. She said that Seth's spirit is still out of balance. She asked me to return to the beach where his soul was separated from his body. I needed to tell him everything, she said, to give his life balance so his death would have meaning. This way his spirit could rest.

"She told me I had to return under the same moon that was overhead when his curse was lifted by the Hessian's silver bullet. She told me how to commune with him." Her gaze lifted to the sky. "The moon is the same as that night. So, I ask you once again, will you serve me, serve him, one more time?"

I didn't know how to respond. At first, I wasn't sure if I believed any of it. But this was no less fantastical than anything else I'd encountered on that journey. If there was any truth to what she was saying, I owed it to Seth. He saved my life more than once. It was the least I could do.

My shoulders lowered, and I let out a puff of air. I walked over to the carriage door and opened it for her. Her eyes sparkled again as she walked over. Before she stepped into the carriage, she reached inside for a dark object that sat on the seat.

She withdrew a black tricorne and handed it to me. It was just like the one I'd lost in the forest during our adventure. Except this one was much nicer.

"A driver should be in a proper uniform," she said with a smile.

I fixed it on my head. "Yes, ma'am," I said as she stepped inside.

When she was seated, I shut the door and latched it. I climbed up into the driver's seat. It had a black leather cushion and some springs under it—a serious upgrade from the other carriage's wooden seat. There was a shiny new brake handle too. And the reins were high-quality black leather. Everything sparkled beneath the moon's light.

I sat there for a moment, taking it all in. The horses shuffled as they waited for my command. The lead horse looked back at me impatiently.

My gaze followed the streetlamps that led out of town. With a reluctant sigh, I shook the reins.

The team started out slow, but soon we picked up the pace. The carriage lamps guided our path. The road led southwest, drifting away from the sea. It didn't take long for us to make it out of Port Calibre.

Waiting beyond the light of the city was the Dark Forest.

The water disappeared as we rode past the tree line, but I could still hear the waves. The road got rougher the farther away we got from the city.

We pushed on for several hours. As we rode through the area, I looked up at the night sky. A million stars peeked through the canopy. A nice breeze came off the water and slipped through the trees.

Despite my fears, I thought about this place from time to time. Whenever I took a job on the other side of the forest, I considered going straight through. But nightmares of the gruesome murders, horrific battles, and narrow escapes always prevented me for doing it.

Yet here I was, taking her back through the land once again. I remembered how I felt when I first picked her up: tired and a little anxious to get going. That uneasy feeling settled in when I first saw the blue eyes.

I peered into the carriage, just like I had that night. Mi Lady was staring at the moon, a gloved hand resting under her chin. It was all so familiar. I turned to look behind us. A small part of me hoped to see Seth's blue eyes one more time. There was nothing but the dark of night.

Time moved quickly, and soon the forest opened. We rode with wide fields on one side and the sea on the other. We arrived at the beach where Seth was killed.

The moon was in its highest position in the night sky. Rays of light shone brightly over the entire beach. As I searched for a good place to stop, it seemed to get even brighter.

I pulled the reins and eased the brake back. The horses slowed down, and the carriage came to a standstill. I locked the brake and hopped down to open the carriage door for mi Lady. She took my hand and stepped out, carrying a large satchel in her other hand.

She looked around, eyes settling on the sea. "The *drabarni* said if I came back here under the same moon, used a candle made from the flower of the red door, and stood with a dream catcher infused with white magic, Seth would appear on the other plane. She said the smell of the red door flower would guide him to me."

Her gaze went distant, as if she were remembering the past. "When we were growing up together in the village, Seth and I would take long rides into the forest. There were times when we just wanted to be alone. Sometimes, I would meet him at the abandoned church in the old village within the forest, the place he took me the night the black wolf's attacked us on the beach.

"We'd meet in the cemetery behind the church, the same place he wanted to be buried. There used to be a stone wall that surrounded the graves. Seth would say it was the safest place to meet, because nobody looks for the living among the dead.

"The entrance has an iron gate intertwined with dark red vines. Their bright red thorns secrete a deadly poison. The iron gates of the cemetery are covered with them. There are so many it makes them look like red doors. It's almost as if they are there to guard the cemetery.

"The vines have dark green leaves and unique flowers. The outer portion of the petals is trimmed in black and tipped with red. Inside, the petals are a bright red.

"The flower has a distinctive smell. Seth always loved the scent. He said it made him think of me. But the vined flower is rare and only grows in certain parts of the forest.

"After I married the governor of Normandy, a few of the servants encountered a beautiful flower in the forest. They nearly died when they accidentally touched the thorns. I knew right away which flower they'd picked. I had the oils from the petals made into a perfume. This reminded me of him, which is why I wear it."

She pulled the hood up over her head, lifted the hem of her dress, and made her way down the beach. She walked to the place where Seth had died. For a moment, she just stood there, listening to the surf crash into the rocks beyond her. Then she wandered a little farther, down to the tide pools.

I stood by the horses, then decided to climb atop the carriage. We were on a small hill, too, so I had a good view of the beach from above. I watched as she set the satchel on the ground. She pulled a candle out of the bag and set it on some rocks. Using some flint, she lit the wick. As it burned, the sweet scent reached all the way to my perch on the carriage roof. It was familiar, though I'd never smelled a red door flower. It was the scent she had carried since the moment she came out of the mansion. It was her perfume.

After the candle had burned for a few minutes, she pulled a large dream catcher from the satchel. Its strings had been woven in the pattern of Seth's tattoos, jagged and crisscrossed like the thatch of a roof.

Standing, mi Lady positioned the dream catcher to capture the moon's rays. As the light shone through, the pattern began to glow the same blue as Seth's tattoos—evidence of the white magic the *drabarni* had infused into the pattern.

The air shifted, and the warm breeze turned cool. As the wind moved through the dream catcher, clouds drifted to cover the moon. The pattern's glow started to fade as the wind became stronger.

Mi Lady's cape flowed behind her. The air vibrated with something indescribable. After everything I had seen, I thought nothing could shock me. But I was not prepared for what happened next.

Mi Lady turned slowly, looking past the dream catcher and down the beach. I followed her gaze. A large, tan wolf trotted up the sandy shore toward her. The magnificent animal slowed his gait to a walk.

She slowly removed her hood. In the candlelight, her eyes sparkled. A warm smile came across her face. The wolf licked his lips as he moved closer, past several tide pools. He stopped just before reaching her, close but out of reach. She extended her hand, but he stepped back.

It was as if he stood in another world. She could see him, but she could not touch.

He looked just like he had in the field so many months ago, except now he didn't have the tattoos or scars. But his eyes still glowed the same blue.

Mi Lady said something to the wolf. I was too far away to catch her words, but I could see tears rolling down her face as she spoke. She had carried the secret of losing their child all her life. But now she was finally telling the only person in the world who mattered.

Time seemed to stand still. And just as it had when Seth was killed, sound died out. I couldn't hear the waves or the leaves of the trees behind me.

My gaze dropped to the large tidal pool nearby. The reflection in the water should have shown the wolf and mi Lady. Her image appeared, but Seth stood in place of the wolf. He was dressed in a long blue coat with a white lining and gold trim. A crimson-colored cloth neckpiece was tucked inside a white shirt. He had gray pants and black knee boots. He looked as handsome as I remembered.

He stood facing her, wearing the same expression I'd seen on his face each time he glanced at her. The look was full of kindness, compassion, and love. He was not angry—together, their love could handle the pain.

My eyes lifted to the ocean for a moment. When I looked back at the tide pool, the image of Seth was gone. Mi Lady stood alone on the beach. The wolf had vanished.

She slowly pulled her hood up over her head. She placed the dream catcher into the satchel and blew out the candle. The wind died down, and the clouds parted. The beach was once again bright with the moon's light.

Before she headed back to the carriage, she scanned the rocks again. Something had caught her eye, but I didn't see anything. Suddenly, the wolf jumped up onto a rock. He stared at her, his long tongue lolling out of his mouth.

A moment later, something totally unexpected happened. A small wolf pup jumped up on the rock beside him! Mi Lady dropped the satchel. Her hands covered her mouth. Tears of joy flowed from her eyes.

The pup's fuzzy fur glistened. It was a dark brown that verged on auburn. My heart lifted at the sight of the wolf pup's eyes. They glowed the same brilliant blue as the larger wolf's eyes.

It yipped excitedly when it saw mi Lady. The large wolf lowered his muzzle to the pup, nudging it. The pup licked the face of the large male and then scampered back down the other side of the rock. The large wolf gave a quick bark and then jumped down. They disappeared out of sight.

Mi Lady stood motionless for a moment, no doubt taking in everything that had happened. Then she picked up the satchel and walked back to the carriage. Every so often, she looked over her shoulder at the beach.

Without a word, she moved to the door. I climbed down from the roof but had to dry my eyes before I opened the carriage for her. She placed the satchel inside and stopped for a moment, letting her eyes drift up to the full moon. I looked up too. It was so large now, a giant in the entire night sky.

When she looked back at me, her eyes were filled with tears. When Seth was killed on this beach, her pain had filled the night air, but she'd never gotten a chance to grieve. Even though the weight of her secret had been lifted, she still had to deal with the loss of Seth.

But at least she had seen him one last time. She had set him free as the *drabarni* had instructed. His spirit could finally rest.

"Here," she said, handing me the dagger of dark silver. "He would have wanted you to have this."

I scanned from handle to tip. It looked as new as when she'd first shown it to me. "Didn't you place this in Seth's hand before the pyre was lit? There isn't a mark on it. The wood handle isn't even singed."

She looked back out over the beach to the spot where she last saw the wolf and the pup. "It's magic."

She took a moment, then stepped into the carriage one last time. "We can go home now."

I closed the door, secured the latch, and climbed into the driver's seat. I took in a large breath as I looked up at the moon. The pain of this life was finally over for Seth. He had done what he always did: sacrificed himself for others, for her. She would live with this pain, but she would live.

I realized the *drabarni* hadn't been helping Seth find peace; she'd been helping mi Lady. She gave mi Lady a way to unburden herself and see what lay beyond. The *drabarni* was restoring the balance to mi Lady for all the suffering she had endured. Now, mi Lady could live her life in peace.

Maybe someday I would be able to tell this tale without ridicule. I might be able to do it without any ale. People might even believe me. For now, it would have to be enough that I knew it was true.

I wept for him. For her. For them. He had loved her more than anything and gave his life for hers—not once but twice. They were robbed by this world and by the black wolf. But they had love, the purest and most precious of gift humans could impart to one another. No measure of time or tragedy could take that away.

As I grabbed the reins, I heard a faint howl echoing through the darkened forest. It was a wolf's song. There was no intimidation or fear in its howl. It was a final cry in the moon's light.

Mi Lady and Seth will return.

# THANK YOU

Thank you for reading this book and coming on the adventure. My sincerest wish is that you were able to escape the world for just a short while and enjoy your time in the Dark Forest. I hope you enjoyed the story and that, despite all the horror, there were parts that made you smile. Readers like you are the reason authors like me enjoy telling our stories.

If you enjoyed the story, please consider providing a short review on Amazon, Goodreads, or any other location. Reviews and likes make the story more accessible to other readers and are invaluable in producing other works, such as sequels.

For more information on future stories, adventures, and other things, please follow me at

 @AlanMcGill14

 @AlanMcGill14

alanmcgill.com
acryinthemonslight.com

You can also listen to an audio version of *A Cry in the Moon's Light* as a podcast at cryinthemoonslight.podbean.com or wherever podcasts can be found.

The story is narrated by me, with original music provided by Joseph McDade. If you like the score, you can listen to it on most streaming services.

# ABOUT THE AUTHOR

**Alan McGill** is an American author who lives in northwestern Pennsylvania with a clowder of cats. Alan was close to his grandparents, who grew up during the Great Depression. They were married young and remained together until his grandmother's passing. His grandfather served in the Navy during WWII and was a gifted storyteller who wove humorous tales about tough events. Alan grew up listening to these stories of right and wrong and watching fictional heroes—such as the Lone Ranger, Adam West's Batman, and Captain America—stand up to bullies and protect those who could not protect themselves. This inspired him to always do what was right in his own life and shaped his love of storytelling. He is a multigenre author whose debut novel, *A Cry in the Moon's Light*, combines horror, romance, and mystery. As with all his books, *A Cry in the Moon's Light* centers on characters who strive to do the right thing regardless of the adversity they face. The book focuses on the theme of love—a pure and deep love that defeats all evil.

If you enjoyed this tale, don't forget to pick up your copy of

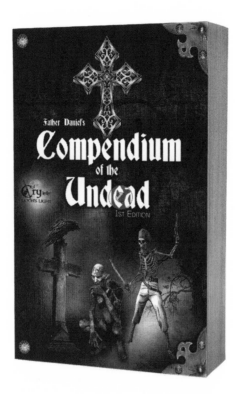

This is the ultimate guidebook to everything *A Cry in the Moon's Light*. Father Daniel (a character from the sequel) is a monk at the Abbey of Feldberg who compiled this book to help fight the hideous creatures of the night. Contained within *Father Daniel's Compendium of the Undead* are over seventy-five illustrations, detailed description and explanations of scenes and places from the story, in-depth character bios, a bestiary, and maps to show you the way. You'll also find glimpses into the characters and places of the sequels, and even a spoiler—mi Lady's full name!